GUIDEPOSTS

CHURCH CHOIR
MYSTERIES™

The Sad Clown Affair

Nicola Furlong

Guideposts®

CARMEL, NEW YORK 10512

www.guidepostsbooks.com

www.guidepostsbooks.com
Guideposts Books & Inspirational Media Division
Series Editor: Michele Slung
Cover art by Stephen Gardner & Edgar Jerins
Cover design by Wendy Bass
Interior design by José R. Fonfrias
Interior cat illustrations by Viqui Maggio
Typeset by Composition Technologies, Inc.
Printed in the United States of America

*Dedicated with love, admiration and gratitude
to my mom, Pat Furlong*

Acknowledgments

I WOULD LIKE to thank Michele Slung, for her plot suggestions and fine editing, and Elizabeth Kramer Gold, for allowing me to continue visiting Willow Bend. And as always, special thanks to Glynne Turner.

The Sad Clown Affair

H E'S LOST *WHAT?*" Gracie Parks asked, holding the
telephone closer to her ear.

She glanced over at her elderly uncle, George Morgan, who
was enjoying his hot lunch: a second helping of Gracie's
hearty corn and cheese chowder along with another thick
wedge of her freshly baked Irish soda bread. She caught his
eye and slowly shook her head. Uncle Miltie, as he was
known to his friends in Willow Bend, stopped eating mid-
spoon and waited.

On the other end of the line, Lester Twomley sighed heavily. "It's very sad, Gracie. He's lost his smile. For a clown,
that's pretty much a career-ender."

Though concerned by her friend's distressed tone, Gracie
couldn't help asking, "Your cousin is a . . . *clown?*"

Gracie's uncle raised his bushy eyebrows in surprise. Then

he grabbed a hunk of bread, broke it in two and attempted to juggle. Gracie was unable to hold back a smile. Her uncle's incorrigible hamminess was the reason he had been nick-named after the old-time television comic, Milton Berle. Uncle Miltie never missed an opportunity to make everyone in the room laugh. Now he managed to catch the bread and once again attacked his chowder.

"Yep," Lester replied. "Has been for over sixty years. I know it sounds a little ridiculous, but when he was just four-teen he ran away from home to join the circus. He hated school, hardly ever went. Anyway, his running off pretty well broke his poor mother's heart. Believe it or not, he's been clowning around under the big top ever since."

He paused to reminisce. "Oh, Gracie, I wish you could have seen his act! Other clowns juggle or do acrobatics or make funny faces, one thing at a time. Not Paddy O'Brien. You see, Gracie, my cousin was small and quick, and always wore a trademark bright green wig. They called him the Leaping Leprechaun. He used to step-dance through the audience while juggling shillelaghs or playing the fiddle and singing 'When Irish Eyes Are Smiling' at the top of his lungs. But now. . ."

Les sighed again. "Well, I just got off the phone with him, and I've never heard him sound so down. He says he just can't laugh or entertain the kids and their families any more. This from a man I've never even seen frown! It makes no sense!"

"Oh, Les, that's awful!"

"It sure is. Unfortunately, he won't tell me everything that's happened, but he did let slip that the circus dropped his act and now he's got no place to live. Imagine! He's given his whole life to that circus and now that he's having some problems, they kick him out."

Her friend took a deep breath, struggling to curb his anger. "Anyway, I've invited him to stay with me for a while, take in some of our fresh Indiana air." He hesitated, then added softly, "I'm hoping he might find some solace in speaking with Paul."

"I'm sure he will," Gracie replied. They both had reason to admire the gentle counseling talents of their pastor, Paul Meyer. Eternal Hope Community Church was fortunate to have him. "I've always found Paul's guidance to be insightful, offering strength and hope in ways I hadn't considered," said Gracie.

Hearing this, Uncle Miltie nodded, then rose to take his empty dishes over to the sink. "You know, Les," Gracie continued, "a little home-cooking probably won't hurt, either."

She could almost hear Lester's breaking smile through the receiver.

"I was hoping you'd say that, Gracie," he said. "There's nothing like a bowl of your rice to bolster the spirits!"

"When does your cousin arrive?"

"Tomorrow afternoon."

"Why don't you bring him to dinner? That is, if he's not too tired...."

"Are you sure, Gracie? That'd be great."

"Of course I'm sure," she replied.

This time Lester's sigh was one of relief. "I can't thank you enough," he told her. "You're going to love Paddy." Then she heard him chuckle.

"What's so funny?"

"I was just thinking about what it'll be like to have your uncle and my cousin in the same town, much less the same room."

Gracie understood. "You think Willow Bend isn't big enough for *two* lovable old hams?"

Her uncle glanced up with a look of mock injury.

"Don't worry, Les," continued Gracie. "I'm sure there's more than enough corn in Indiana for the two of them."

Uncle Miltie winked happily at Gracie's large orange cat, Gooseberry, who twitched a whisker and ignored him.

Gracie spent the rest of the afternoon cleaning house. Since she regularly vacuumed, dusted and polished, a light touch-up was really all that was required. Still, once she began, she ambitiously decided to wash the inside of all the windows and polish the kitchen floor. As her adored mother used to tell Gracie and her brother Buddy whenever they rushed through their chores, "Remember, dears. If something's worth doing, it's worth doing well."

Her uncle pitched in as usual, but his osteoarthritis meant he wasn't as agile as his niece. And yet, sometimes, on good days, he could put an entire cleaning crew to shame.

Gooseberry was engrossed in his own tidying-up. Perched above the living room couch, he meticulously ran a raspy pink tongue over and over his plump body until the pumpkin-colored fur gleamed in the pale afternoon light.

Gracie enjoyed being active. Exertion followed by seeing the result was very satisfying. And as she worked, the repetitive labor of the tasks allowed her mind to wander freely. Sometimes, she pondered the mysteries and challenges of everyday life, while at other moments she sought spiritual support or guidance.

On this particular March afternoon, while a north wind shrieked skiffs of snow across her partially bare front lawn, Gracie was letting her thoughts run free. She found her thoughts soaring with "Ring the Bells of Heaven," a joyful anthem that her choir had practiced for the first time just recently.

Although the group had varying musical tastes and singing experience, they were generally open to learning new selections, as long as they had plenty of time. With Barb Jenning's capable direction and talented accompaniment on Eternal

Hope's old organ, singing the good Lord's praises at their beloved church's second Sunday service was always a loud, joyful and mostly harmonious event.

As she mopped, Gracie Lynn Parks found the urge to sing too strong to resist. Pushing and pulling the mop in four-four time across her kitchen floor, she let loose with a jubilant rendition, ending in a powerful chorus. "Glo-ry! Glo-ry! How the angels sing: Glo-ry! Glo-ry! How the loud harps ring! 'Tis the ran-somed ar-my, like a might-y sea, Peal-ling forth the anthem of the free!"

She noticed a movement out of the corner of her eye. Turning, she saw her uncle, soiled duster in hand, leaning against the door jamb. "Don't let me stop you, dear," he said, smiling fondly at her. "I don't think I've heard that one before. It's very uplifting."

Gracie smiled back at him. "That's all I know, I'm afraid. Marybeth brought it to our attention at the last practice. It's called 'Ring the Bells of Heaven,' and it was one of her father's favorites. I'm not sure I know all the words yet, but it's certainly spirited!" She lifted the mop and plunged it into the bucket of suds. "Well, I'm pretty well done in here."

Running a hand through her red curls, she glanced at the kitchen clock, then continued, "In fact, I think we're just about finished, don't you? Why don't you sit down and I'll fill the kettle? It'll take a while for this floor to dry, so how about we have our coffee in the living room?"

"Sounds good to me." Her uncle ran his eyes across the sparkling kitchen counter to the large crockery jar where Gracie stored her homemade cookies. "Any of those chocolate chips left?" He licked his lips. "After all this housework, my batteries need recharging. A few chunks of chocolate should do it."

Gracie chuckled. "Is there ever any time it wouldn't?"

"Of course!" the octogenarian replied indignantly.

Hands on the mop, Gracie waited.

Uncle Miltie was silent. She could almost see his mind turning. Suddenly, his face brightened with a triumphant smile and he declared, "When I'm sleeping!"

FOR THE LOVE OF MIKE!" Paddy O'Brien exclaimed in a surprisingly deep voice. He jumped to his feet as Gracie set the main dish—a pork roast on a bed of saffron rice mixed with sage, pepper and olives—onto the dining room table.

Gracie's other male guests, Lester Twomley and Rocky Gravino, flushed, then quickly stood. Marge Lawrence, Gracie's best friend and next-door neighbor, watched from her seat with amusement. Uncle Miltie, who was returning from the kitchen, hesitated while trying to control a grin. He took a step and laid a large bowl of steamed green and yellow beans beside the pork roast.

"I haven't seen a meal like this since I was a lad!" Paddy's wizened face stared at his hostess with wonder.

Just as Lester had said, his elderly cousin was small and

wiry. Though slightly hunched in his old suit, Paddy moved quickly and with ease. Gracie could imagine how light he would be on his feet and hoped someday she might see him dance. He appeared to be in good health, still slender and agile though well into his seventies.

Yet his eyes troubled her. Although a beautiful color—a startling bright green—they sagged deep in his skull, lacking the sparkle and life that Gracie instinctively knew had once flourished within them. She wondered what had happened to dampen their light and what it would take to rekindle Paddy's inner flame. She had promised Lester that neither she, nor any of the other guests, would question him tonight. *Please, dear Lord, help this man,* she prayed silently. *He's obviously troubled and hurting and in need of Your support and guidance.*

"Ta, dear lady, thank you for taking such trouble for a useless old man," Paddy was saying.

"Nonsense!" replied Gracie quickly. She reached over and patted his thin arm. "No one under the eye of God is useless, no matter what their age."

"That's right," Uncle Miltie added as he returned to his seat.

"We're very pleased to have your company, Paddy. Very pleased." Gracie looked at her other guests. "We're happy to have all of you with us this evening, aren't we, Uncle Miltie? Especially on such a cold night."

"You bet," her uncle said.

Paddy's face brightened a bit. "Thank you. You know, Gracie, you remind me of my dear sister, Mary Eileen, sadly departed some ten years ago. She was also very kind, a great cook and a redhead to boot!"

Gracie thanked him with a warm smile.

Uncle Miltie turned to their guest. "Has Lester told you, Paddy, that I'm a bit of a funny guy myself? I can't wait to tell you some of my jokes. How about this one? What do you call a guy who eats meat, vegetables and potatoes?"

Lester groaned, Rocky bit his lower lip and Marge studiously avoided Gracie's eyes.

Paddy shook his head. "I don't know."

Uncle Miltie nodded, then declared dramatically, "Stu." He grinned. "Tasty little punchline, don't you think?"

Thank you, dear Uncle Miltie! thought Gracie. A little humor goes a long way to lighten a weary heart. Even "corn" is nourishing, she thought, smiling to herself.

She glanced with satisfaction around the table, highlighted by flickering candles and the large bouquet of spring flowers provided by Rocky. She paused when her eyes fell on him. The salt-and-pepper haired widower who was the editor and publisher of the *Mason County Gazette* had been friends with both her and her dear husband Elmo, before Elmo's tragic death in a car accident.

Since that terrible time, their friendship had deepened. Yet though she greatly enjoyed Rocky's character, company and counsel, she was not interested in expanding their relationship any further. At least, not yet.

She allowed her gaze to wander. Her uncle sat at the head of the table. Lester and Paddy were standing on her left and Marge was seated beside Rocky, to her right. Perfect. "Please, everyone, sit down."

The men instantly dropped into their chairs.

"Rocky, would you do the honors?" she asked, handing her friend the carving knife and fork.

Lester pushed the roast platter across to Rocky as he returned to his feet.

"*Whoa* there!" Surprised, everyone glanced down at Uncle Miltie. "Wait a minute, Gracie," he continued. "Just because Rocky cuts words for a living, doesn't mean he automatically knows how to carve a roast."

Rocky paused, knife in the air. "Guess you have a point," he said, expertly slicing into the roast. "However, you'd be amazed at the number of things a newspaperman learns on the job. In a previous lifetime," he added, forking perfectly even pieces onto a platter held by Marge, "I even reviewed restaurants. It was actually a chore, though, and their cooking couldn't hold a candle to Gracie's, the fanciest ones included."

He paused. "I'll have you know, Uncle Miltie, that I actually once interviewed a master chef about carving meat." Rocky waved the knife. "It's all in the symmetry between the wrist and the elbow, you know," he continued, sliding his right arm in demonstration.

Lester and Marge applauded. Paddy smiled. But still only for an instant.

"Well," Uncle Miltie admitted, "we've survived your slicing before. The job's still yours."

Rocky bowed briefly and quickly completed his task.

"Before we eat, please let us give thanks," Gracie said, folding her hands and bowing her head. The others followed suit—even Rocky, for the sake of politeness. Gracie knew he held the belief that prayers belonged in church, which he attended infrequently and solely for her benefit.

Lester glanced at his cousin. "How about saying your mother's Irish prayer?"

Paddy's lips tightened.

"Come on, Paddy," Les continued. "I'm sure they've never heard it before. It's really special."

Paddy sighed, then asked softly, "May I, Gracie?"

Gracie looked up in surprise. "Of course. Thank you."

"As Lester said, this is a prayer from the old country that my mammy used to say before we broke bread." The wiry man took a deep breath. "May God give you for every storm, a rainbow. For every tear, a smile. For every care, a promise, and a blessing in each trial. For every problem life sends, a faithful friend to share. For every sigh, a sweet song, and an answer for each prayer. Amen."

"Amen!" the others echoed, diving quickly into their meals.

"That was lovely!" exclaimed Marge. "You Irish really have a way with words!"

"Yes, you do," Gracie added. "Thank you, Paddy. That was beautiful."

In between chews, her guest flashed her a gap-toothed grin. Gracie was delighted to see the shadows of pain in his face disappear. Sadly though, his eyes remained dull.

"Is the *Gazette* covering the budget stuff tomorrow night?" Uncle Miltie asked Rocky, while handing around the platter of beans. "From what I hear, there may be some very unpopular decisions." He reached for some rice. "It's the cutbacks in social programs that have me worried. Most of us older folks are living on fixed incomes and can't afford new expenses."

Marge nodded. "You're not the only ones in their sights. They're going to raise our business taxes *again*." She put down her fork and crossed her arms. "I know everything's more expensive these days but I'm getting tired of them always hitting the business owners first. Our costs are going up the same as theirs."

"I know what you mean," Lester said, cutting into a slice of pork. "My business license has doubled in the past three years." He chewed for a moment, swallowed, then added, "I guess I wouldn't mind them cutting some programs, if it saves me a little."

"I, for one, don't envy the town council's job," said Gracie, scooping rice onto her plate. "You have no idea the pressure they're under." She shivered. "When Elmo was mayor, he had to make decisions that would have stumped even King Solomon himself!"

Her uncle tapped his fingers in agreement. "You're right, Gracie. Everyone's demanding more services, but no one wants to pay for them. The government's got to cut costs wherever they can."

Rocky raised his eyebrows. He winked at Paddy. "I don't know why I bother to pay reporters, when I can just sit here eating a first-class meal, and get all the local buzz for free."

The others laughed, and everyone continued to eat in companionable silence.

"Say, Paddy, speaking of cost cutting," began Uncle Miltie a short time later, "are you getting your Social Security benefits deposited directly to your bank? The Social Security Administration is always suggesting that I do it, claiming that it's safe and convenient but more importantly, they say that it saves them the cost of printing and mailing the check." He paused. "I'm not so sure I trust the system. How about you?"

Paddy swallowed slowly, then shook his head. "*Uh* . . . I don't trust them either." He turned to Gracie. "Do you think I could trouble you for another piece of meat?"

"Of course!" Gracie offered seconds, which all four men accepted immediately.

"This is a brilliant meal, Gracie!" said Paddy, a few minutes later. "Brilliant."

"If brilliant means what I think it means," Rocky added, "then you're absolutely right." He raised his glass in salute. "To Gracie. Thank you."

The others followed suit.

"It's not over yet," Uncle Miltie proclaimed. "There's still an apple pie to come."

Lester and Rocky clinked glasses.

Marge rose to help Gracie clear the table while Uncle Miltie tramped to the kitchen to put on the coffee. Gracie was pleased to see that he wasn't using his aluminum canes. Funny how sometimes the cooler, dry winter weather acted as a balm to his achy joints. Rocky joined them in the kitchen a minute later. "Anything I can do?"

Gracie handed him the pie. He nodded for Marge to precede him with a tray of mugs and plates, then marched behind her into the dining room.

Paddy's eyes watched Marge as she laid out the dishes. "So, Mrs. Lawrence, you're not just another pretty face, but a businesswoman?"

Marge blushed, then instinctively fussed with her hair. "Marge, please. Yes, I . . . *uh*, I have a little gift shop. Despite what I said about resenting more taxes, I wouldn't ever want to stop owning my own business." She smiled. "And you? You must have enjoyed being with the circus. Lester was telling us that you've been working as a clown for over sixty years."

Les shot Marge a warning look, but it was too late. Gracie and her uncle returned just as Marge finished speaking. Her words dropped into a dead silence.

Paddy O'Brien swallowed hard, then lowered his eyes.

Marge flushed redder. "Oh dear! I'm so sorry if I've said something—"

Paddy sighed heavily, but before he could speak, Lester jumped in, his voice higher than usual. "I'm so sorry, Paddy. She didn't . . ." His voice trailed off uncomfortably.

Paddy raised his hand. "It's all right," he whispered, blinking back a tear. "Please, just forget it."

In the ensuing awkwardness, Gracie busied herself with serving coffee. Relieved to have something to do, everyone quickly tucked into their slices and sipped from their steaming mugs.

"I bet you know this one," Uncle Miltie began, looking at Paddy. "What's the customer say when his bank manager tells him he's overdrawn?"

Paddy finished his coffee and nodded. Gracie was glad to see that he appeared interested. "That's impossible," Paddy replied. "I've still got five checks left!"

Uncle Miltie grinned.

It was Paddy's turn. "How about this one? What did the

lady say to the cab driver when he told her that her dollar tip was an insult?"

Everyone looked at Uncle Miltie. He paused, then widened his blue eyes and asked in a high-pitched voice. "How much should I tip you?"

Paddy nodded. "Another dollar."

Uncle Miltie leaned forward and shook his head. "Oh no," he squeaked. "I wouldn't dream of insulting you twice."

Rocky and Lester burst out laughing. Marge and Gracie exchanged amused looks.

The two old clowns grinned, each delighted to have found a fellow jokester.

Paddy turned to his hostess. "You know something, Gracie? Put a red nose and wig on this fella and he'd have them laughing in the aisles."

As Uncle Miltie puffed up his chest and told Marge and Rocky that they had underestimated his talents, Lester looked at Gracie and mouthed the words *thank you*.

For the first time that evening, Paddy's eyes sparkled, albeit very softly.

3

THE COLD WINDS PERSISTED, swirling across the still frozen lawns of Willow Bend, Indiana. The townsfolk reluctantly put aside all thoughts of an early spring, and continued to swathe themselves in heavy coats, thick scarves and warm knit hats.

It was still dark two mornings later when Gracie tugged on a pair of thick-soled boots, wrapped a long muffler around her neck and face, and tramped onto the crust of snow carpeting her front porch. Gooseberry dashed ahead, oblivious to the ice crystals underfoot, his thick coat providing perfect protection from the harsh elements. The light of the fading moon glistened, casting a warm yellow glow across the dips and valleys of the remnant snow bank that still curled against Gracie's front fence.

For a moment, she tried to imagine the scene in spring.

Flowers everywhere! Was it possible? It seemed unbelievable. It was, as Emily Dickinson might have said, a zero-at-the-bone kind of day.

Jamming her gloved hands into the deep pockets of her long parka, Gracie carefully crossed the icy deck and stepped onto the concrete path. Her breath rose in tiny lightbulb-shaped clouds that were ripped into pieces the moment she exhaled. On the sidewalk, encircled by the halo of a nearby street light, she turned back. Her house, its large windows mirroring the dark sky, stood sturdily there against the glacial gusts. Jagged icicles lined the eaves, like a row of shadowy incisors. Drifts of snow piled up along the house's east side, while her prized rhododendrons and hydrangeas peeked out from their protective burlap shrouds on the northwestern corner.

It was hard to imagine that just two weeks ago, Willow Bend had been blessed with a warm spell. All but the thickest mounds of snow had disappeared, puddles had begun to form under eaves, and shimmers of green shoots poked from garden beds. The townsfolk started to shed layers and rummage through garden sheds and garages, actually stopping to chat with one other, instead of the usual winter pantomime of offering a courteous nod while dashing through the chilly air into their toasty warm homes.

But the premature spring fever broke ten days later with the arrival of a massive Arctic front, what Uncle Miltie

"Do you need an ambulance? Should I call 9-1-1?"

"What? Oh, no, nothing like that, Gracie."

Gracie breathed with relief. "What's wrong?"

"Anna just got off the phone with Mary Thayer."

"Oh." She and Anna regularly received calls from Mary, the town librarian, to let them know that one of the they had reserved—in Gracie's case, usually a mystery novel—was in. In Anna's case, it was new audio books.

"Anna's in a terrible state, Gracie. Mary's news hit her hard."

Gracie's throat tightened. "What's wrong?"

From his seat at the kitchen table, her uncle watched her closely, his broad face full of concern.

"What?" shouted Joe again. "Oh. It's not Mary."

This is ridiculous! thought Gracie. I still haven't a clue as to what's going on. She took another deep breath. "Joe? Why don't you let me speak to Anna, okay?"

"I don't think she'll come to the phone. She's too upset."

"Why?" Gracie asked patiently.

The elderly man exhaled in exasperation into the phone. "Well, because of the cutbacks, of course."

"Cutbacks? What cutbacks?"

"Didn't I tell you? Sorry, dear. I thought I did. It happened like this. Mary called to tell Anna that the library was no longer going to buy and carry audio books. You see, Anna had just ordered a bunch of new ones. Mary said that the town council had made the decision to cut the library's funding last night. You know how much she enjoys those tapes, Gracie." His voice dropped to a whisper. "Especially since she can no longer see well enough to read. She's working on learning Braille, but it's awfully hard at her age."

Gracie winced. "Yes." Gracie knew all too well how much Anna Searfoss loved and lived for the written word. A retired librarian herself, Anna had once written a series of children's books that had recently been reprinted. "I'm sure there's some mistake, Joe. A lot of people in town listen to audio books. I see them taking them out all the time at the library."

"You know it. I know it. Mary knows it. But she said the decision's been made and there was nothing we could do. When Anna put the phone down and told me, I immediately thought of you. If anyone can make them change their minds, it's Gracie Parks, I said to myself. Listening to those tapes is one of the few joyful activities left to my Anna."

His voice dropped again. "We can't afford to buy them, Gracie. I doubt many folks who need them can either."

Gracie felt a surge of anger. "Nobody who needs them should have to buy them, Joe." Her voice rose. Her uncle leaned closer. "Nobody! That's what a library is all about. There must be other items to cut from the budget."

"So you'd think," he said. "That means you'll help?"

"Of course she will!" roared Uncle Miltie, banging on the table.

Gracie jumped, and so did the sleeping Gooseberry.

I DON'T MEAN TO BE CRITICAL, Mary," Gracie said, softening her tone so as not to put the librarian on the defensive, "but how did you make your decision to pick audio books as the area to cut? People like Anna Searfoss really need this service. They don't have options like the rest of us."

"I know," Mary Thayer replied, her troubled expression proving that she was uneasy about the decision. "It wasn't easy."

The library was humming with late-afternoon activity. A couple of older men were scanning the newspapers, a number of people wandered about the stacks or tapped keys at the computer reference terminals, and the activity room down the hall echoed with children's voices. After briefing her uncle completely following Joe Searfoss's telephone call, Gracie and he had agreed that her first step should be to speak to Mary Thayer in person.

"After all," Uncle Miltie had advised his niece as she bundled into her outerwear, "no sense in beating around the bush. You might as well go straight to the horse's mouth."

A mixed metaphor, perhaps, but Gracie had agreed with its basic sentiment. Within fifteen minutes, she had warmed up Fannie Mae, her old blue Cadillac, and had driven through town to the low building that housed the popular public library.

An elderly man now approached the check-out computer counter and handed Mary several books about the Second World War, as well as two audio books. Gracie stood aside as the librarian smiled and quickly processed the articles.

"Now, where was I?" she said, moving away to let another librarian take over. Gracie slid along the other side of the counter until the two were near the front doors, far enough away not to disturb anyone.

"Oh, yes, the audio book decision. Well, as I said, Gracie, it was truly difficult. It's a well-used program, but then what isn't? We had already been warned by the council that if certain cuts were approved, we would be expected to 'reduce our service levels immediately.' In anticipation, all the library staff got together a couple of weeks ago and we went through our budget and our services."

A tiny woman, with a thick scarf wound around her head

and face like a mummy, came through the front doors. Gracie braced as a gust of chilly air swirled in along with her.

"Oh, hello, Mrs. Thompson," Mary said cheerfully. "It's a cold one, isn't it? Here, dear, I'll take those if you'd like."

The woman peered up at her from behind foggy glasses, then stared directly at Gracie before carefully handing over a pile of well-worn fashion magazines. "You're not going to keep on chatting and forget them, are you?" she asked querulously. "They're all due today. I don't want to have to pay any fines."

Mary smiled. "Of course not. Why don't I just check them in right now, okay?"

Silently, Mrs. Thompson waited.

Mary flashed Gracie an amused look, then stepped to the keyboard to complete her task. When she was finished, Mrs. Thompson nodded, then headed to the magazine rack, still as wrapped up as when she'd entered.

"She's such a dear," Mary said, returning to her stool. A frown suddenly creased her brow.

"What's the matter?"

Mary shook her head. "It's just that she's not going to be very happy when she finds out that we've decided to cancel our subscription to her favorite magazine. It's one of the old-fashioned ones, and most of the women prefer the newer, more modern magazines."

Mary sighed. "You see, Gracie, over the past few years, we've had to take on a number of new services, like offering the computer terminals, training sessions and access to the Internet."

Gracie nodded. Although Gracie remained an Internet neophyte—mostly just using email to correspond with her son in New York—Uncle Miltie had dived into the new digital world, gotten his own personal computer and now surfed the web with the ease and interest of a teenager.

Mary continued, "We were given most of the funding to purchase the equipment, and the rest we had to scrounge out of other areas. But we received nothing for the support—which can be a lot."

"I know," replied Gracie, glancing over at the bank of computers, each one in use. Hardly a day went by without her uncle complaining about some error message or software crash his home system experienced. "A lot of time seems to be spent fussing around computer screens these days. I'm not convinced that this dependence on so-called high technology has made our lives that much better."

"You and me, both." Mary laughed. "Well, anyway, getting back to our meeting, we went through all our services—you know, buying books, newspapers and magazines, hours of operation, training courses we provide, that sort of thing. We ranked each one in order of priority. Unfortunately, the purchase of audio books isn't anywhere near the top of the list. Besides, we already do have a considerable existing collection."

As though to reassure Gracie, Mary added, "As I just said,

the audio books aren't the only things being cut. We'll have to scale back a number of our magazine and newspaper sub-scriptions and think twice before ordering new hardcovers. It's the new reality. I don't like it, but. . ."

Gracie nodded. She understood the pressure that public and social services were under these days. Still, she remained determined to try to help her friend Anna.

"Is there any other way? The people who check out the audios all the time like to have new ones, obviously."

Mary grimaced. "I wish there were, believe me, but I can't think of one. We went round and round, trying to come up with some new cost-saving ideas. We're running pretty close to the bone as it is. Last year, we had to cut back on our part-time help, just to save enough money to pay for the introductory Internet classes."

Mary looked at Gracie. "If you think of anything, please, let me know. I'm not looking forward to the reaction once these cuts are a done deal."

"Aren't they already in effect?"

Mary shook her head. "We submit a list to the council next week. It's mostly a formality, but as of today, we're no longer buying new audio books and a lot of magazine subscriptions."

"How much do you have to save?"

A group of book borrowers suddenly descended on the desk. The other librarian glanced at Mary in a silent but obvious plea for assistance.

Mary tapped her fingers. "About five thousand dollars all told. I know it's not a huge amount, but we sure can't find it here. And even if by some miracle we got a few thousand, I'm not certain we'd be able to allocate it to the audio books. Look, I'm sorry, Gracie, but I need to help out. Please, like I said, let me know if you think of anything."

Gracie promised she would and stood for a moment, watching the half dozen patrons receive their books. Only one person was taking out an audio book. Five thousand dollars, she thought, exhaling slowly. Far more than she had ever imagined. She pushed open the door and stepped into the frigid air.

Well, dear Lord, where there's a will, there's a way, right? I've just got to find that way. I've got the will, and I know I've got Your support. What more can I ask?

"Five thousand dollars!" exclaimed Uncle Miltie, as they began dinner several hours later. He was so shocked by the amount that he dropped his fork. It clattered onto the kitchen floor, narrowly missing Gooseberry.

Gracie spooned broccoli salad onto her plate and grinned. "Breaking into your piggy bank won't help."

He raised an eyebrow. "You undoubtedly have a plan—it only has to be legal!"

Gracie shook her head. "I'm not sure how to approach it, actually. It seems to me there might be at least two options:

somehow raise the money or change the library's priorities."

Her uncle nodded. "Well, I'm relieved you're not contemplating robbing a bank—red-haired ladies usually get fingered in line-ups, and there's hardly a soul in Mason County who doesn't know you."

He looked at her, then added, "What about the town council? After all, they're the ones who initially made the decision to cut the library's budget. Maybe we could convince some of them to change their minds."

"Public opinion means most in an election year, and this isn't one."

Uncle Miltie finished eating, then pushed his plate away with a sigh. "Well, whichever way you tackle it, dear, it's going to be a lot of work. People, especially those with political power, don't take too kindly to folks second-guessing their decisions."

Gracie nodded. "I remember that happening on more than one occasion during Elmo's terms as mayor. Making waves is never easy."

"How did El handle it when people did that?"

Smiling at the memory, Gracie replied, "Calmly, as always. He welcomed public input, at any stage of the decision-making process, and he worked hard to make sure that the townsfolk understood how the council had arrived at its decisions."

She rose and carried their dishes to the counter. "There

were times when El felt it was appropriate to order a review." She reached for two small plates. "Brownie?"

Her uncle looked at her, startled. "You have to ask? I'll get the milk."

The phone rang just as he bit into a rich chocolate square.

"I'll get it," said Gracie. She wiped her hands and reached for the receiver. "Hello?"

"Did I catch you in the middle of dessert?" a familiar voice asked.

Gracie laughed, delighted to hear from her only child. "Your timing's perfect, dear. Uncle Miltie's halfway through a brownie, as we speak. How nice of you to call. Is everything all right? Wendy? Little Elmo?"

Arlen Parks chuckled. "Everything and everyone's fine, Mom."

Gracie slipped into a nearby chair. Her uncle was gesturing at her with half a brownie. "Your great-uncle says hello, or rather he's waving a brownie to that effect."

"Too bad he can't slide it through the phone. My mouth waters at the thought of one of your brownies. New York has some great ones, but none as good as yours!"

Gracie teased, "It must be the Indiana water! Everything I cook tastes better to you than what you find in New York!"

"What can I say?"

She adjusted the receiver to fit more comfortably on her shoulder. "Is there any chance you might be able to take some time off and come down? I know I sound just like a mom, but. . ."

Her son sighed. "I know. We were hoping maybe Easter. . ." Gracie's heart leapt. ". . . but Wendy's spring recital is the following weekend and she'll be tearing her hair."

"Then why don't just you and Elmo join us? We'd love to see her, of course, but if she's going to be working. . . ."

For a moment, Arlen was silent on the other end, then he replied, "As always, you're the best. Give me a chance to talk it over with her, okay?"

Thank You, dear Lord, for offering me this wonderful possibility to look forward to.

"Now, it's your turn, Mom. Tell me how it's going down there. Are you feeling okay? Did Uncle Miltie win any more contests?"

She smiled at her uncle, who was gulping the last of his milk. She noticed two brownies had already disappeared. "I'm fine, dear. As for your uncle, his luck hasn't been very good lately. But that doesn't stop him from trying though."

"I wouldn't expect anything less!" Her son chuckled. "How about the gang? Marge? Rocky? Abe? The choir? What's gone on this week?"

"Well, we had Lester and his cousin over for dinner a few nights ago, along with Marge and Rocky. A lovely man named Paddy O'Brien. Unfortunately, he seems to have experienced some recent unhappiness. Lester says he lost his job, but he thinks there's more to it. Paddy won't talk about it. Lester's hoping that in the peaceful atmosphere of Willow Bend he'll open up, perhaps even confide in Paul."

"You never know," Arlen replied. "What's he do for a living?"

"That's the really sad part, dear. Paddy's a circus clown, or at least he was. He doesn't seem to want anything to do with it now, not even talk about it."

"Wow! A real clown, you say? What a shame! Little Elmo would go crazy over him, asking a thousand questions. Come to think of it, I can't even begin to guess what it must be like to live and work in a circus." Arlen then paused, his tone turning serious. "Something pretty bad must have happened for him to feel so negative, Mom, don't you think?"

"I'm afraid so, son."

They talked about the mystery of Paddy's seeming misery for another couple of minutes, and, after that, Gracie gave Arlen all the news of her closest friends. When she brought up how devastated Anna Searfoss was because of the library cutbacks, Arlen whistled.

"I'm not surprised, Mom. The same kind of stuff is happening here. You should organize a petition right away."

"A petition?" Gracie hadn't thought of that.

"*Uh huh.* You know, collect a bunch of signatures from folks who are against the council's decision. If you get enough of them, and—this is very important—if you submit them while the issue's still hot, maybe the town will reconsider. You've got to get your position out quickly, though, so folks will understand why you're appealing. Otherwise, they may not trust you or believe what you're trying to do."

"A petition! What a good idea!" Working on another brownie, her uncle now glanced up with interest. "Thank you, Arlen!" Her thoughts were racing ahead. "Well, if you don't mind, dear, I'm going to hang up and get started right away. Give my love to Wendy and my precious little grandson."

"Looks to me, my girl, as if you've got a plan," her uncle observed when she'd hung up.

"I'm thinking it over . . . a petition, *hmmm*."

Uncle Miltie nodded thoughtfully. "I like the sound of it."

"Then you can give me the first signature!"

"Point me to the dotted line!"

5

GOOD GRIEF! What will they think of cutting next?" Pastor Paul Meyer exclaimed the next morning after Gracie had told him about both decisions made by the town council and the library. He invited her into his small study, near the back of Eternal Hope Community Church, and gestured for her to sit down.

"Many of our congregation enjoy listening to those tapes, Gracie. You know that! It's hard enough that those folks who most need the audios are frequently the infirm and the shut-ins, the ones with lives that most need brightening and the distraction of good stories read aloud!"

When Paul Meyer first arrived in Willow Bend, some townsfolk had been taken aback by his youthful zeal. It didn't take long, however, for his congregation to discover that the sandy-haired newcomer was conscientious, considerate and kind. Now he was one of the town's most admired citizens, and one of its most loved, as well.

"That's right, Paul," said Gracie. "I've often picked up or returned tapes for several of our shut-ins, so I know what you say is true. That's why Uncle Miltie and I spent last evening coming up with this brief statement, telling people about the decisions and about our goal to collect five hundred signatures within the next two weeks. Or as many more than that as we can. We're hoping all the local churches will, as an act of fellowship, put it in their bulletins or, even better, make the announcement at their next service. And Rocky will place it in the *Gazette*. Maybe he'll even run a story that can help shine a light on the situation."

She sat back and shook her head. "Why, just the other day when I was dropping by the senior center, Molly Cook had her residents gathered round to listen to a tape of *Anne of Green Gables*. Oh, Paul, I wish you could have seen those women's faces! It was as though they were back reliving their childhoods!"

She vowed suddenly, "We can't let something like this happen without a fight!" Her eyes flashed.

Paul looked at her affectionately. "The petition is a great idea. But how about we take it one step further? Once we collect the signatures, why don't we deliver them in person at the next meeting?"

Gracie didn't hesitate. "That's an excellent suggestion, Paul! We could easily fill the council's chambers with our supporters." She paused, imagining the scene. "I think if we can get everyone behind us, they'll have a tough time ignoring the issue."

She went on, "I just wish I had more experience with this sort of thing. We don't have a lot of time, and we need to make every minute count!"

Paul looked at her admiringly. "You've already done a good deal. We're all going to pitch in!"

Gracie looked at him gratefully. "Would you be willing to call the pastors of Bethesda Methodist and the Evangelical Free Church and let them know what we're trying to accomplish? I'll contact Dr. Ebersole at Waxmire and Susie Frantz. She sings in Trinity's choir."

Paul reached across for the copy of Gracie's announcement. Scanning it quickly, he said, "So, you want the volunteers to call you directly?"

Gracie considered this. "*Hmm*, I'm not sure. To be honest, Paul, I'm open to suggestions."

"Let me think about it." He smiled encouragingly.

"Well, as I said, Uncle Miltie and I went over it last night," said Gracie, "and tried to imagine how it would work best. I think what's best is if I can arrange for several individuals to join me immediately on an organizing committee. Each of us will be responsible for a number of volunteers and an area of town to canvass."

Paul nodded. "So, maybe the first thing to do is to pick your committee members? Once you've got them organized, they can help you get the word out." A smile crossed his lips. "Maybe I *can* be of some help."

He leaned forward. "If you don't mind my saying so, Gracie, what we need here is someone seasoned at organizing meetings, who handles committees and deadlines and fields phone calls as a matter of course. And, who would offer to help without the slightest hesitation."

There was indeed one, and only one, individual in their congregation who met Paul's criteria perfectly. Gracie looked at her pastor, hope shining in her eyes. "Are you thinking about the same person that I'm thinking about?"

He grinned. "Yep."

Gracie nodded.

"Pat!" Paul sang out.

The church secretary, Pat Allen, immediately appeared at the door, notebook in hand, pencil at the ready. "Yes?"

They both grinned at her. Paul waved her inside.

"How would you like to help Gracie take on the town council? It'll involve organizing a whole bunch of folks to canvass every door in town. The idea is to solicit signatures for a petition. All for a very good cause, of course. Do you think you could manage it?"

Pat didn't hesitate. She glanced between Paul and Gracie, then smiled. "Just fill me in on the details. If you two are for it, then I'm your woman!"

Pat quickly turned one of the Sunday School classrooms into her operations center. Almost before Gracie and Paul could sit down, she had written Audio Books Coalition across the blackboard.

Paul now taped up a comprehensive street map of Willow Bend. He glanced at Pat's heading. "*Hmm*, I like that, Pat. It makes for a great acronym: ABC."

Gracie nodded. "Hey, and it makes me think of a slogan, too. 'Signing our petition's as easy as ABC, and it's the right thing to do!'"

Pat said, looking at the map, "I think it makes sense to group the rural areas together, since they'll have to be tackled by car."

Examining the map carefully, they decided that it could be sensibly divided into eight sections. Using a red felt marker, Pat drew a line around each. No one knew exactly how long it would take someone to cover a street, but when Gracie mentioned that she power-walked three miles in roughly fifty-five minutes, they figured it would require five or so people several hours or more to knock on every door in any one section.

They also realized that canvassing the neighborhoods closer to the center of town would be accomplished more quickly than those in the outlying areas. They decided to stick with their approximate calculations for the moment.

If necessary, changes could be easily made later.

Their next task involved brainstorming a list of possible names to head teams, in addition to Paul and Gracie.

"While you two are making calls," said Gracie, "I'll use my cell phone and get onto some local businesses. Perhaps there's something they can do to help."

Pat said, "Excellent." She turned to Paul. "I suggest we try and get individuals who can come to a meeting here, say tomorrow night around seven?" He nodded.

"I'd be happy to bring something to munch on," Gracie offered.

"Thanks, Gracie," Pat said.

Paul now momentarily disappeared, but returned, clutching his jacket and keys. "Okay. I'll be back in an hour or so." With his list tucked in a pocket, he headed off to use his home phone.

Gracie left Pat in her office and slipped back into the classroom to make her calls. Through the half-frosted windows, she caught a glimpse of swirling snow flakes and moved closer to the door. She could easily have pushed up the heat but decided not to waste the energy since she would be using the room for less than an hour.

"Well, hello, Gracie!" Rocky's voice boomed moments later into her ear. "Is this a dinner invite?"

Gracie chuckled. "Not officially, but you know you're always welcome to drop by."

"*Whew!* But what can I do for you?"

"I'm meddling in the council business, but for an awfully good cause."

He whistled appreciatively. "Sue attended the meeting and is still fine-tuning her piece. Our phone's been ringing off the hook, Gracie! A lot of folks already know much of what the council decided and are none too happy. I've asked her to do a follow-up, as well." He paused for a moment. "But what are you doing about it?"

"I guess you could say that I'm one of those unhappy folks." She told him about the Searfosses' phone call and the efforts since undertaken. "I was hoping that you might consider sending one of your staff over to speak with Anna and Joe to find out just how important audio books are to the blind. Maybe also speak with Mary Thayer at the library. She can give you some specifics about the number of people—not just the ones with vision problems—who enjoy listening to audio books. I think this way you'll get exactly the sort of reaction you're seeking."

Rocky whistled again. "Sure, Gracie. But Sue's already got enough on her plate, so I'll get Mike on it right away. Hang on a minute, okay?"

He hollered for Mike Struthers, then Gracie heard his

muffled voice giving instructions. Next, Rocky yelled for his photographer, Ben Tomlinson. She could tell he was being dispatched to Anna and Joe's.

"Now, how about your petition, Gracie? Mike will need to cover it."

Thank You, dear Lord, Gracie was silently praying. *And thank You for Rocky understanding the urgency.*

She replied, "That's great!"

"Now, to change the subject. I've been thinking a lot about Les's cousin since we met at your place."

"Oh dear. No!" she replied, feeling a pang of guilt. "Since I talked to Joe, I've been so wrapped up in getting this business going, I almost forgot about Paddy. I was intending to try and learn more about what's troubling him."

"Hey Gracie! Don't beat yourself up! Even you can't expect to help everyone every minute. Look, I'm sorry I brought him up. I didn't mean to make you feel bad."

"That's all right, Rocky. I'm just glad you reminded me. I do want to see how he's doing." She paused. "You said you had been thinking about Paddy?"

"Well, about his life, really. I mean, the guy was a circus clown! That's just plain neat, don't you think? I've never known a real clown before, have you?"

"Nope, me neither."

"I've been sitting here, trying to imagine what it must be like to spend your whole life in a circus. Doesn't it make you curious?"

She chuckled.

The newspaper editor's voice now was excited. "Paddy's biography would be a grand story, don't you think? All those circus people, moving from place to place but never staying long enough to really visit or learn about it. They'd miss everything we take for granted, like the familiarity of our hometown, listening to the local radio station, why even going to the same dentist, year after year."

He took a breath. "These circus folks don't really have a home base, ever. I guess you'd say they're our version of the gypsies. Hey, now that's an interesting angle—*uh* . . . hang on again, okay, Gracie? I'll be right back."

A second later, Gracie heard his voice, now muffled. He talked to someone for half a minute.

"Sorry about that," Rocky said, voice clear again. "Just a layout problem. Now, where was I? Oh, yeah, as I was saying, circus people don't have regular lives like we do."

Gracie murmured agreement.

"Not only that, their actual jobs are so unusual!" he continued. "Most of us work nine to five. Paddy's old pals tame and train tigers for a living or fly through the air on a trapeze! And he earned his living wearing makeup and weird clothes and tripping over his feet, just to make children laugh. Think about it! What could be more fun?"

But it's also possibly very lonely, Gracie thought suddenly. She said, "It would be a good story, that's for sure. I just don't think Paddy's ready to tell it yet."

Rocky sighed. "Yeah, I guess you're right. He seemed down, that's for sure. Of course, that's the way most of these comics are."

"What do you mean?"

"Well, you remember the old song about the tears of the clown?"

"I do."

"You understand then that being funny is a way for some people to cover their pain. Making others laugh is a way to avoid facing one's own troubles. I'm not saying all clowns are actually unhappy guys but...."

The frightened face of a chubby boy flickered into Gracie's mind. My goodness, she thought, I haven't thought of him in years! "I once knew a boy in the fifth grade named Hermie Hilson," she told Rocky. "He was new, and overweight, and almost everyone teased him. One day at school, I came down the hallway and around a corner. And there he was. Backed up against a wall by several other boys. He was shaking, absolutely terrified."

"What happened?"

"It's odd. I was about to call out for help, when suddenly Hermie started talking. But, it didn't sound like his own voice at all! It was amazing. He sounded just like our teacher! He was impersonating him perfectly!"

"What did the other boys do?"

"Nothing at first. Then they laughed. So did I. From that day on, I guess you could say Hermie was the class clown."

"See what I mean?"

"Yes, but that doesn't mean that Paddy O'Brien is like that. From what Les says, his cousin's always been an optimistic person. It's just lately he's been gloomy."

"Okay. It would just make for a better story, that's all. Well. . . ," he added, reluctance suddenly creeping into his voice, "I guess I should let you go. I'm sure you've got a lot more calls to make."

"That's true, I do."

"Just remember to keep me posted on any developments!"

"I promise. And you promise me, Rocky Gravino, not to run away and join the circus!"

"Okay, okay," he agreed. "Not this week, anyway. It's too interesting seeing what's going to happen here in Willow Bend."

GRACIE'S NEXT CALL was to Charlie Robertson. The congenial owner of Robertson's Pharmacy was indignant.

"I can't believe the council's decision, Gracie. Dottie and I listen to audio books from the library all the time when we're traveling." He paused. "I wish I could help with the canvassing. Unfortunately, we're doing inventory every evening this week and much of next. Is there anything else you'd like from me?"

"Well . . . would you consider donating some paper? Those signatures have to go on something!"

"Done! Where and when do you need it?"

Gracie told him gratefully, "Thanks, Charlie. I could swing by later and pick it up, if that would be convenient."

"*Uh uh.* You don't have to do that. I'm happy to drop it off on my way home tonight. All right?"

"That's very kind of you."

He snorted. "Kind nothing! It's the least I can do. Oh, and Gracie?"

"Yes?"

"Any chance you could send someone to the pharmacy instead of to our home? As I said, we're here every night, and we sure don't want to miss the chance to sign!"

Gracie chuckled. "Done!"

Next, Gracie called the Searfosses and told them about her plan and to expect a call from the *Gazette*. They were delighted and immediately agreed to being interviewed and photographed. Gracie couldn't help smiling as she overheard Anna asking her husband to drive her to the beauty salon before she hung up.

Then she left messages asking for support on the answering machines of her fellow choir members. When it came to Les Twomley's machine, she added that it would be terrific if his cousin would like to help out. She wanted to say that she thought it might be good for him to get involved and meet people, but decided it was safer to tell that to Lester in person. It was very possible that Les might listen to his phone messages in his cousin's company.

Her last phone call was to Marge, who answered the telephone at her gift shop on the first ring.

"I know all about it from Cordelia," her friend said upon hearing Gracie's voice. "Pat called her just as Cordelia was heading out to come by here and pick up a present for her niece. I think it's shocking, Gracie. Absolutely shocking! My mother loves those tapes. She goes through them as fast as you go through mysteries."

Marge sighed. "I certainly can't afford to buy her enough new ones to keep her happy. Especially now that they've raised my business taxes."

She paused to take a breath. "Of course, I'll pitch in and canvass! Just let me know where and when. Is there anything else I can do?"

Gracie pondered for a moment. "Other than telling everyone who comes into your shop, I'm not really sure." She then told Marge about her conversation with Rocky. "The newspaper piece will reach a lot of people, but. . . ." Another idea had struck her. "Would you put a flyer in your front window? That way we can reach even more people!"

"Of course, I'd be delighted to. And I bet every business on Main Street would be equally willing. Look, I've got another suggestion," her friend continued. "When I was in Mason City doing a little Christmas shopping last year, I signed a petition to protect some historic buildings from the wrecker's ball. And you know where I signed it?"

"No. Where?"

"In that sweet little dress shop on Front Street. The petition sign-up sheets were located right beside the cash register! So, why couldn't we do that right here in Willow Bend? It would give our residents another opportunity to participate, in case they aren't home when your volunteers drop by."

"That's a wonderful idea, Marge! Do you think the other shop owners would be willing to do that?"

"I don't see why not, especially if the right person asked."

"You mean me?"

"Of course. There aren't many people in this town who'd ever turn you down, Gracie Parks, when you're on a goodwill mission. I'm sure if you dropped by, you'd have no trouble finding takers. Oh, before I forget, Cordelia asked me to tell you that the members of the Historical Society are willing to help out. She said just to give her a call when you get the chance."

"Wonderful." Gracie couldn't help thinking, as she often did, how blessed she was to live in Willow Bend. "Well, Marge, I'd better go. I've got more calls to make. Thanks again for the great suggestion. I'll keep you posted."

"Wait! Before you go," Marge quickly shouted just as Gracie was about to hang up. "What about Barb's party?"

"Oh, dear! Thanks for reminding me. With all this petition stuff, I almost forgot." Gracie paused for a moment. "As far as I know, everyone's coming."

"Great! I, for one," Marge said, laughing, "can't wait to see what the guys'll end up wearing!"

Gracie responded, "We really shouldn't be laughing. We still haven't decided on what we're going to wear."

"Oh, I've got that all figured out. I'm going with a sailor theme. You know, like in *South Pacific*?" She giggled. "You've got to admit, Gracie, that'll be cute!"

"Cute's what Uncle Miltie's afraid of!"

Marge Lawrence giggled again. "And I was thinking, since you're the one with red curls. . ."

Gracie groaned. It was too obvious. "Oh, no! Not *Annie!*"

Marge retorted, "You bet your Daddy Warbucks!"

Sighing, Gracie replied, "Okay, but promise me one thing."

"Yes?"

"That I don't have to sing that song."

"What song?" asked Marge innocently. She paused, then said, "Oh, you must mean, *Tomorrow, Tomm*—"

Grinning, Gracie hung up to the sound of her friend belting out the famous show tune.

GRACIE NEXT DIALED the barbershop and told Barry, the proprietor, what had happened and what they were hoping to accomplish.

"I'd be pleased to put up one of your flyers, Gracie," the barber responded. "As to the petitions, I'm good for those, as well. I don't have a lot of space near the register, but I'll rustle up a little table or something. And if you'd like to leave some extra flyers with me, the guys can read them while they're waiting their turn." He chuckled. "It'll make a nice change from my old copies of *Field & Stream*."

In quick succession, Gracie called several more businesses. Each owner agreed to posting flyers and sign-up sheets. Young Hammie Miller, of Miller's Feed Store, surprised Gracie by being an aficionado of audio books, claiming to listen to more than one western novel a week while doing his deliveries. He even went so far as to offer to tape a flyer to the back window of his van and to stuff one in every bag.

She was just about to dial the number for Abe's Deli when Pat knocked on the classroom door. The church secretary was holding two steaming mugs. Gracie waved her in.

"Thought you might need a cup of tea," Pat said, handing one of the mugs over. "Oh, my word, Gracie! I can almost see my breath in here. Why didn't you turn up the heat?" she asked, heading to the thermostat.

"Please, Pat, don't bother," replied Gracie. "Honestly, I'm fine. I'm not going to be in here long enough to justify it."

"Are you sure?"

Gracie nodded, her fingers wrapped tightly around the mug. She gratefully sipped the hot beverage.

Pat perched behind a desk in the row beside her. Gracie bit back a smile, as she imagined this forty-something woman as a keen fifth grader.

"How's it going?"

Gracie replied, "Pretty good, so far." She relayed the results of her several conversations.

Pat nodded. "Marge's suggestion is excellent. We should be able to catch a lot of people." Then she frowned.

"What's wrong?"

Pat pursed her lips. "Well, I'm not sure how we're going to be certain that people don't sign the petition more than once. We sure don't want to have to go through the names one by one. Any duplicate names and there goes our legitimacy."

Gracie hadn't thought of that possibility. The two women sipped in silence. Finally, Gracie said, "What if we tell everyone just that? We can clearly state on the petition that each person is allowed to sign only once and that double signatures could lead to a disqualification of our petition. We could also ask our canvassers to make sure the people they solicit haven't already signed a petition in town."

Pat nodded again. "I think that would do the trick. That reminds me, we've got to put our heads together to design both the flyer and the sign-up sheets." She leaned back against the hard chair. "It would be nice to have the assistance of someone better at graphics than I am. Any ideas?"

"Rick Harding," replied Gracie immediately. "Of course. Hang on, I'll give him a quick call!"

The handsome African American answered his office phone on the second ring. "Why, hello, Gracie! Some problem with this week's practice time?"

Among the choir members, Rick was known for his soaring tenor as much as for his sense of humor and willingness to help.

"No change, as far as I know. I'm calling about something completely different." Gracie briefed him, then mentioned the requirement for the flyer and petition sheet layouts.

"It'll be a snap, Gracie. Do you need some help?"

Gracie smiled happily at Pat. "Yes. We do."

"No problem. Why don't you just jot down what you want? I can swing by the church or your home whenever it's convenient, chat it over with you and then make a draft for you to review. How's that?"

"Perfect! I can't thank you enough."

"Don't mention it, Gracie. When Lily was a baby, we couldn't get her to sleep. I don't mind telling you that my wife and I were going crazy. Then one night, purely by accident, Comfort was listening to an audio tape while rocking the baby and Lily fell fast asleep! We realized that she was lulled by the sound of the narrator's voice. After that, we were hooked on audio books! We've listened to them ever since."

Gracie asked him if he could come by her house later that evening. Rick agreed, then just before he hung up, he added, "Oh, don't forget to sign me up as a canvasser, Gracie. I'll bundle Lily up in her snowsuit and pull her around in her sled. That'll give her mama an evening or two off."

Yes, dear Lord, thought Gracie. *I can sense Your support in every phone call I make. Thank You!*

By the time Paul returned, the women had prepared a draft of both the sign-up sheet and the petition. Paul skimmed them, then nodded in agreement. "I'm glad you make mention of the fact that we only want one signature per resident." He cleaned his glasses, still foggy from the change in temperature.

Gracie and Pat looked at each other with a sense of mutual accomplishment.

"So," the young pastor said, edging into one of the student desks, "I've got four volunteer team leaders and nine canvassers. How'd you do, Pat?"

"Not as well as you, but well enough." She grabbed a piece of chalk, drew eight columns across the board, then on two columns she scribbled the name of a team leader as the title. "Two leaders and five canvassers. I've requested them all to call their friends and neighbors and ask if they can help out."

Paul nodded while reading the board. "Molly Cook and Phil Murphy. They'll both do a good job."

Gracie agreed. As the director of the local senior center, Molly was a skilled coordinator. Phil taught music and was in charge of the high school band, and somehow, every year, he managed to shape a group of adolescents into a harmonious team.

Paul tugged a wrinkled piece of paper out of his jeans. "You can add Marybeth Bower, Cordelia Fountain—who says the whole Historical Society will volunteer—Ken Ebersole and Susie Frantz to round out the list of leaders. Oh, and Ken offered to do some photocopying."

Gracie couldn't have been more delighted with the other four. Marybeth, a mother of twins, had a heart of gold and a work ethic of steel. An inordinately proud tourist home owner in her seventies, Cordelia would pitch in anywhere, anytime, when the well-being of senior citizens was threatened. Kenneth, a doctor of divinity and the pastor of Waxmire Tabernacle, was known as a charismatic speaker. And lastly, it was Susie's fine organizational skills that allowed her to successfully home-school her children, as well as participate in a number of activities in town.

Paul handed Pat the slip of paper. "These are the others who've agreed to canvass."

While she jotted down the leader's names, Gracie peered over Pat's shoulder and ran her eyes over the rest of Paul's list. Their volunteers now numbered into the double digits!

8

SINCE PAT STILL HAD TO FINISH a number of administrative tasks for the church, and Paul had previously scheduled a visit to the local hospital to visit several patients who were members of his flock, Gracie picked up the slack. She decided to swing by the pharmacy for the copy paper and save Charlie the trip to her house. She and Paul left the building for the parking lot.

"Oh, Gracie, I've been meaning to ask," Paul said, hiding the top half of his face with one gloved hand. "What do you think of me as The Phantom?"

Gracie blinked momentarily.

"For Barb's party."

Understanding hit home and Gracie grinned. "*The Phantom of the Opera!*" She laughed. "Why, Paul, it's not what I'd call typecasting, but it's definitely going to get a reaction!"

He grinned back. "It's going to be fun to see whom everyone else comes as."

Gracie had to swallow a smile. It really was hard to imagine this gentle young man as the disfigured and menacing lunatic who haunted the old Paris opera house.

Gracie then wondered, "Have you met Lester's cousin, Paddy O'Brien, yet?"

"No," he replied. "But Les called me a couple of nights ago and filled me in."

"He's not sure if his cousin will talk to me, but it seems Paddy's agreed to be here on Sunday. I guess he hasn't been in church in a long time, so at least it's a start." He paused thoughtfully. "I'll personally welcome him, of course, but I think it's best to let him come to me."

Gracie nodded. "I hope he can find his way to talking to you. He's very sad, and, I think, a little scared."

He looked at her. "That's not surprising. He's in his seventies and he's just lost the only job and family he's known for decades."

"Yes," said Gracie. "Of course. I'd be terrified if I were in his shoes."

"We've got to remember that Paddy's lived a very unusual, nomadic kind of life. Very different from the rhythms and ways of our little town."

"Yes," replied Gracie, remembering her recent conversation with Rocky. "The things we take for granted, like having a permanent place to live, staying and becoming involved in one community, these are things he hasn't experienced. Everywhere he's gone, he's been a stranger, except in the circus family."

"Let's hope he will let us welcome him as one of us and let us be part of his new family." Paul tugged at his wool cap. "The evening he spent in the warmth of your house was a first step."

The roads were swept bare, save for the occasional chunk of ice left behind by the snowplow. In no time, Gracie was maneuvering into a parking spot next to the pharmacy. As she hurried along, a man called out her name. Gracie turned and waited while the mayor of Willow Bend dashed across the street.

Gracie had been involved in her share of municipal issues, and had appeared before Tom Ritter and the town council on a number of occasions. She considered Tom to be a fair-minded mayor, but wished that, now and again, he spent more time asking for advice and comments from the average citizen.

"I'm glad I've run into you, Gracie," said Tom, catching his breath. "Could we go somewhere warm, have a coffee and talk?"

"It's about the audio book petition?"

He nodded. His cheeks were red and his breath hung in the air. "We've already received a pile of complaints about our budget decisions." Tom shrugged under his heavy tweed overcoat. "Not all of them in support of your position, I'm afraid."

Gracie wasn't surprised. She knew that with any political topic there were always at least two sides. Her beloved Elmo used to say that if folks weren't passionately for or against an issue, it was almost not worth the town council even considering it.

"I'll even buy." Tom glanced in the direction of the deli.

Gracie teased, "Are you thinking of bribing me? If so, I want a cheese danish."

Tom gave her a thumbs-up.

Once inside, they were bathed in a yeasty-smelling warmth. Abe looked up from behind the cash register, greeted them cheerfully, then nodded in the direction of an empty booth. "Be right with you, folks."

Tom helped Gracie remove her coat, then hung it on a hook with his own before slipping into the seat opposite. He sniffed. "*Umm*, something sure smells good." Then he shivered. "Whatever happened to spring? I put this coat away two weeks ago and had to get it back out again!"

Abe arrived with a pot of coffee and two mugs. He was now sporting a bright yellow pair of earphones, and a small tape player hung from his apron. Tom groaned good-naturedly. Abe slipped off the phones to ask, "I'm sorry, Tom. Did you say something? I was just listening to the new Dick Francis. Don't you just love listening to books on tape?"

Gracie swallowed a giggle. Tom raised his hands in mock surrender, while Abe flashed Gracie a grin and poured. While they sipped, Abe said, "In the future, Gracie, would you please tell your uncle to keep his weather predictions to himself?"

Tom glanced quizzically between them.

The delicatessen owner continued, "This latest cold front is all his fault. He told me last fall we'd be having unusual weather patterns in March."

The mayor's eyebrows shot up in surprise. "I didn't know your uncle was a meteorologist?"

Gracie smiled. "He's not. He's just addicted to the *Farmers' Almanac*."

"Good thing there isn't a jokester's almanac!" Abe told them. "He'd be really impossible to hold a conversation with!"

They all chuckled, then Tom asked, "What's that incredible smell?"

"Pecan rolls. Fresh from the oven."

Tom glanced at Gracie, who nodded. "We'll each have one, please. You can have the danish to take home, Gracie."

While they ate, they talked politely about noncontroversial matters like the newest baby in town and a variety store that had just closed its doors in Mason City. Finally, Tom got back to the subject they'd been avoiding. "How did you come to be involved in this?" Tom asked curiously.

"I received a call from Joe Searfoss. You know Anna's losing her sight?" He nodded. "Well, audio books provide her with great stimulation and company. I decided that something should be done about it."

"The library's decision to stop purchasing them isn't the town's fault. We didn't tell them what to cut." He leaned forward, placing his hands upon the table. "Come on, Gracie, you know what it's like. We're getting hit with new demands every day. If it's not one thing, it's the other."

He sighed.

"You don't approve of our taking matters into our own hands?"

"Listen, Gracie, each and every citizen has a right—practically an obligation in my view—to make sure that the elected officials represent his or her position. It's just that . . ." He fiddled with his coffee spoon. "I'm not sure how we could have come to another conclusion. We can't fund everything. Besides, like I said, we didn't tell the library what to cut. They made that decision."

"Yes. A decision forced by *your* cutbacks." Gracie leaned forward. "Look, Tom, all we're doing is asking the residents to tell us if they support the council's proposed cuts. They don't have to sign the petition if they don't agree with it. However, if enough people feel a review is in order, don't you think you guys and the library staff should know about it?"

Tom shook his head. "Obviously, Gracie, I can't disagree with you. We are here to serve the public, after all."

Abe approached to refill their mugs. "Oh, and Gracie, bring one of those petitions by as soon as you can," he said innocently. He gave a big wink. "I bet everyone who comes in here will sign it." He paused, the pot hovering tantalizingly above their empty mugs. "Especially if they want service." Another wink.

Tom Ritter rolled his eyes.

Gracie and Abe began to laugh.

MAY 6, 1840."

In amazement, Gracie stared across the kitchen table at her uncle. To his right, a pile of old envelopes tottered precariously near the table's edge. Nearby, an old album he had found in her attic was flopped open, its pages of dulled and curled plastic still protecting a smattering of fading stamps. *"Eighteen-forty?"* She shook her head. "It's hard to imagine that the English had a postal service back then, much less one that required stamps. How about here at home?"

Uncle Miltie informed her, "We started using stamps seven years later." He put his spoon down. "In five- and ten-cent denominations."

While Gracie finished her last bite of nutmeg-dusted custard, he continued telling her what he'd learned about stamp collecting. She was delighted to see him so absorbed.

There was nothing her uncle liked more than learning the background of some new pursuit that interested him. He had been holed up in the attic all day, rummaging through old boxes and trunks. He'd even had the inspiration to phone Paddy O'Brien and invite him over in the morning, thinking the distraction might be welcome while Les was out working.

Gracie wasn't sure what *plate book*, *selvedge* and *hinged stamps* all meant, even after he'd explained. But his excitement and enthusiasm were enough to keep her listening contentedly.

She was also a little tired from the petition chores. Fortunately, she had finished her remaining phone calls right after returning from Abe's. Everything was set for tomorrow's meeting with the team leaders, and Rick had swung by before dinner to pick up the petition and poster drafts. Now, Gracie leaned back, savoring the peaceful moment and her uncle's enthusiasm.

"Scarcity and condition," Uncle Miltie was saying as he put a glass carefully into the dishwasher. Gracie guessed that he was quoting something he'd read while surfing the Internet. "Those are the two most important factors in determining phil . . . uh . . ." He paused, leaning on one of his aluminum walking sticks, "phil-a-te-lic value."

"*Hmmm,*" she said. She gave him the rest of the cutlery. "So, age isn't a factor?"

Here was an easy question. He grinned happily. "Well, it

used to be that any stamps issued after the nineteen thirties were considered modern and not collectable, but that's all changing. Anything in good condition from the thirties and forties is worth buying. Lots of people collect stamps. Did you know Field Marshall Rommel was an avid collector?"

Gracie shook her head.

"Makes the enemy seem more human, don't you think?"

"I suppose so," she replied.

"I'm especially interested in the era around World War II." He looked pensive. "I guess seeing them brings back memories, good ones. . . ." He absent-mindedly touched one of the envelopes. ". . . of the letters Doris sent me."

Gracie's breath caught in her throat. She knew many men who had served during the Second World War. Some spoke openly and freely about those horrific days, while others refused to discuss them. Her uncle talked easily of his general experiences during that war but was less forthcoming about the time he'd been incarcerated in a prisoner of war camp.

Suddenly, Uncle Miltie gripped the old airmail paper in his gnarled hand as though it were a precious talisman, and stared fiercely into his niece's eyes. "You can't imagine, Gracie, how good it felt to have a letter from Doris in my pocket, in my hands! To read her own words and know that she was out there, safe, and waiting and praying for me . . . in the midst of that . . . that awful camp . . . all the noise, and pain and death."

Tears shot into his eyes. "Oh, dear . . . I miss her so."

Gracie's hand enveloped his closed fist before her own hot tears burned her cheeks. She squeezed hard, startlingly aware of the contrast between the roughness of his skin and the smoothness of the thin paper. Gracie felt ashamed. She knew how often she thought of her own beloved Elmo and how keenly she still felt the pain of losing him.

Dear Lord, please forgive me for my blind selfishness! I know that my wonderful uncle mourns his wife deeply, but I'm never quite sure if I should make more of an obvious effort to provide comfort or not. Men can be so proud sometimes! He's such an independent and capable person, and I would never want to cause him any unnecessary pain or embarrassment.

Please help me to be more considerate and to recognize the times when he might require my sympathy. I know that it is through Your grace and blessing that I have him in my life, and for that I am truly thankful. Let him know that I am here for him whenever he needs me.

Neither spoke. After a few moments, her uncle sighed. Gracie removed her hand, wiped her face with a tissue and smiled at him. "She's still waiting and praying for you."

He blinked away a tear and nodded. Then he looked affectionately at his niece. "She's not the only one on my side, I know. Thank you, Gracie."

Thank You, Lord!

"One of the Fetislov lads—they're the high-wire act, you see—owned one of them . . . gizmos the kids carry around . . . *uh* . . . boom boxes," Paddy was saying to her uncle when Gracie returned from her shopping expedition.

She hesitated, pleased to hear the newcomer chatting so easily and not wanting to interrupt. The weather had improved overnight, and she had taken advantage of the thaw to tackle a list of errands around town.

"It had a radio and a tape machine. He was mad for westerns, was Sergei, ever since he was a boy in Minsk." Paddy pretended to shoot Uncle Miltie, who collapsed and flopped dramatically in his chair. Paddy blew away the imaginary smoke from the barrel.

Like a pair of schoolboys, they grinned at one another.

""He couldn't read English," continued Les's cousin, "so he bought audio books. Zane Grey. Anything with a cowboy or a horse on the cover." Seeing Gracie's face, Paddy jumped up and practically ripped the screen door off its hinges to let her in. Gooseberry streaked out into the late morning light.

"Top of the morning to you, my lovely lass!" He took both grocery bags out of her hands and set them carefully on the kitchen counter.

"Thanks," she told him. "It's nice to see you again."

"Paddy's agreed to help out with the petition," her uncle said. He winked at her when the other man's back was turned.

Gracie's expression remained unchanged. She knew the

wink was her uncle's way of intimating to her that Paddy would agree to do anything if Gracie was involved.

"That's great."

Paddy blushed. "Our Les told me about the situation." He shrugged his thin shoulders. "As I was telling your uncle, we used to listen to a lot of tapes at the . . . circ . . . *uh*, the job. It helped pass the time while we were moving from one town to the next."

Without warning, Paddy's face crumpled. He stood very still, struggling for composure. For a long moment, Gracie feared the elderly man would actually cry. It was obvious that his pain remained very near the surface. She held her breath.

With perfect timing, her uncle poked a thick thumb toward a plastic bag slouched against one of the kitchen chairs. "Look what Paddy brought with him."

Gracie blessed him silently. "What's that?"

Paddy, his cheeks pale but his composure returned, explained. "They're from Les's basement. I told him about Uncle Miltie's new hobby and, quicker than a pixie, he nipped down and rooted out these old letters. Seems they've been sitting around since before Adam was in short pants. He said that if we find anything of value, it's ours."

Gracie was pleased to see that Paddy was alert to ways to make himself liked and useful. He obviously wanted to be her uncle's friend, too, and that had to be a good sign.

"Paddy, won't you stay for lunch?" asked Gracie. "We're

only having tomato soup and tuna sandwiches but there's more than enough...."

Her guest appeared torn. There was caution tempered by yearning in his expression. "You're sure I'm not being a pest?"

"Of course not," replied Uncle Miltie. He grinned and now was the one pretending to aim a six-shooter. "Gracie lets me have friends over all the time. *Bang!*"

There were chuckles all round.

After lunch, the two men cleared the table, then examined their loot. With an armload of cookbooks and a fresh pot of tea, Gracie settled into the living room. Later, she planned to make coconut-walnut squares and oatmeal-and-raisin cookies for the petition meeting at the church. Gooseberry padded along the top of the couch, registered that she had books in her lap, but stared expectantly at her, anyway.

Gracie shook her head. "Sorry, old boy, but I've got me some work to do." She patted a nearby spot. "Come on over here, instead."

The cat leaned toward her sensuously. Gracie scratched him until he began purring. Seconds later, Gooseberry was curled into an orange ball and snoring lightly. With the comforting low rumble of male voices in the background, his mistress sipped her tea and looked for recipes for Barb's party. Since she and Marge were planning to serve just finger food and desserts, she wondered how it would work if she named the dishes after their Broadway theme. For example, *Showboat* shrimp spread or *Carousel* cheese canapés. She flipped to the desserts. Why not a *Sweeney Todd* torte?

Gracie was still giggling at this last thought when the phone rang. Gooseberry's eyes popped open momentarily.

"I'll get it," called Gracie. "Hello?"

"Thank you, Gracie!" a man shouted.

Recognizing the voice, Gracie replied, "You're welcome, Joe. May I ask what you're thanking me for?"

"Anna's thrilled."

"About what?"

"What? Don't you know? But, I thought you sent them."

Gracie inhaled slowly. Sometimes Joe Searfoss could be so exasperating, always jumping ahead in his conversations. "Sent who, Joe?"

"Why the reporter and photographer from the *Gazette*, of course. Didn't you send them?"

"Not exactly, dear. Remember, I told you that I spoke to Rocky Gravino, the editor? He sent them."

"They just left. They asked how long she'd been listening to audio books, how much it meant to her, oh, all kinds of questions! And when I told them my Anna was an author and showed them her books, well, they couldn't believe it. I thought everyone already knew."

His voice faded. Gracie could just hear that he was saying something to Anna, then he was back on the line. "What do you think, Gracie? How they could miss knowing about our most famous writer beats me!"

"Since the paper covered the story, I think it's probably just that they forgot."

"Oh, I see," he said slowly. "Well, it's good they were reminded, then. They even took photographs of her, holding her books. She's just so excited."

Gracie smiled. "I love hearing that she's so happy, and I'm sure the article and photos will be a big help to our efforts." Somewhere nearby, her cell phone rang. "I'm sorry, I've got another call. I'll keep you informed, okay? Bye, Joe!"

"I tried the house line but got your voicemail," Rocky Gravino said after she had rummaged through her bag and located the ringing phone, "so I figured your uncle was on the Internet. Just wanted you to know that we'll be running the Searfoss piece in tomorrow's paper. Is your meeting still on for this evening?"

"Yes. Is Mike still coming?"

"He'll be there, don't worry. I hear Tom Ritter bought you coffee yesterday."

Gracie shook her head. News travels fast in a small town. "He did."

"What did he want?"

Gracie hesitated, uncertain whether she wanted to see the details of her conversation with the mayor in print.

"Off the record, then." She was glad she remembered to stipulate this.

"Okay, okay."

"All I asked him was to accept that some people might want the council's decision reconsidered."

Rocky chuckled. "And...?"

"Well . . . he knows it's our right, but I'm sure he'd be a lot happier if we didn't continue with our petition."

"Unfortunately, he's not the only one. We're starting to get calls and letters and e-mails defending the town's position."

Gracie sighed. She had considered the possibility that the petition wouldn't be unanimously popular—nothing ever was—but she had hoped that those opposed to it would try to understand why it was being circulated before they began clamoring against it. Her side still needed to get their position out to the citizens of Willow Bend.

"Don't worry, Gracie," Rocky continued, reading her thoughts, "after tomorrow's edition hits the streets, folks will know exactly what you stand for and why you're appealing for their support."

Gracie wasn't so sure. Arlen's words echoed in her head. He had said, "You've got to get your position out quickly, though, so folks will understand why you're appealing. Otherwise, they may not trust you or believe what you're trying to do."

She was a little worried that it might already be too late.

I'LL HANDLE THAT ROUTE, if you'd like," said Phil Murphy. "My van's pretty comfortable."

Pat Allen briefly considered his suggestion, then replied, "Thanks for the offer, Phil, but if you don't mind, I'd rather use you in town."

Paul Meyer stood near one wall, with his back to the map of Willow Bend, which he had earlier tacked up. He turned and wrote Phil's name across the area in a thick red felt pen.

Gracie glanced up from her notes and smiled. The meeting was going perfectly. Neatly tucked in an envelope lay Rick's drafts of the petition and sign-up sheets, which he had dropped off just as she was leaving for the church. She was delighted with the clean and simple layout, but what had struck her the most was his clever use of an unusual block capital font.

Now, each petition sheet and information flyer was headed by the catchy ABC logo. The large colorful letters, which resembled children's building blocks, immediately reminded her of books and reading. Perfectly suited to their cause!

Since the volunteers were all briefed on the issue and also flexible, the assignment of leaders to geographic areas was taking far less time than anticipated. She was glad Pat had put coffee on just before their meeting began. The comfortingly ordinary smell was just beginning to fill the room. Gracie noticed Marybeth Bower and Cordelia Fountain glance longingly over their shoulders toward the table where she had laid out the sweets, alongside the now-bubbling percolator.

"So," said Gracie, "that leaves areas seven and eight still unclaimed?"

Pat nodded.

Someone knocked on the door and a man stepped briskly into the room. "Hi. For those who don't know me, I'm Mike Struthers. From the *Gazette*. Okay if I join you folks?"

"Be our guest," replied Pat, gesturing to an empty seat.

After he was settled, Molly Cook suggested, "If you don't mind, I'll gladly take number seven. It includes the senior center which allows me to collect signatures during the day."

"I was hoping you'd offer, Molly. Thanks," Pat said. She looked questioningly at Kenneth Ebersole.

The pastor of Waxmire Tabernacle rose slightly. "That leaves number eight to me."

"If you don't mind? I know it requires more driving."

He waved a large hand. "Suits me, Pat. I'd enjoy an outing in the country."

"Excellent! Thanks." Pat checked something off on the paper in front of her. "Okay, I suggest we start canvassing this Saturday."

Phil frowned. "That's only two days away. Aren't we jumping the gun just a little? I mean, we'll barely have had the time to tell folks what we're trying to do."

Paul nodded. "I'm with Phil. Remember, Pat, the church bulletins won't be available until Sunday. They're one of the main ways we're advertising in the community."

Pat paused to chew a pen. "I take your point. However, the sooner we get the petition to the council, the better our chances of making any impact." She glanced around the table. "I'm open to suggestions. What does everyone one else think?"

"Monday," suggested Susie. "For one thing, it's usually a quiet night, for family activities, I mean. I think we'd catch a lot of folks at home."

"I agree with Susie," Molly offered. Cordelia and Kenneth nodded in unison. "Most people do their shopping on Saturday so I'm afraid we'd miss a lot of them when we come by."

"Tuesdays aren't bad," said Phil. "Nobody ever does much on a Tuesday."

Gracie started to say what Rocky had told her, about the stirrings of negative response, then decided not to.

Pat looked at the rest. "Any other comments?"

Mike stuck up a hand. Pat nodded and he said, "I hope you don't mind my butting in, but my piece will undoubtedly run in Saturday's edition."

Phil shot a look aound the table, as if to say, "See? I told you so!"

Pat's shoulders dropped slightly. "Well, I guess we start on Monday."

Phil's satisfied expression withered under Pat's sharp stare. She continued, "We'd better plan for Tuesday evening as well." She jotted a note to herself then glanced at her wristwatch. "I think the coffee's ready. Why don't we have a short break, then we'll assign you the names of those who've volunteered so far. Gracie, will you please hand out Rick's drafts?"

Gracie nodded and reached for the envelope. "These are examples of the design for the petition and sign-up sheets. If you'd all take a quick look and give me any comments before we leave tonight, I can start the ball rolling so we can have them pronto!"

They all stood up. Before she could make it to the coffee, Mike cornered Gracie. "Can I ask you a few questions?" He had a small pad at the ready.

"Sure."

"You're masterminding this petition, right? But why are *you* so upset about the library's decision to cut back on purchasing audio books? Do you listen to them, yourself?"

Gracie paused to collect her thoughts. "Of course I do!" She shrugged before continuing. "The trouble with the decisions about budget cuts is that they were made without consulting any of us who are affected or who do care!"

"Sure, but isn't that why we vote for those folks on the town council? To have them make those kind of decisions for us?"

The others in the room were now listening intently. Phil opened his mouth to comment, but shut it immediately after receiving a surreptitious elbow in his side from Cordelia Fountain. Phil coughed to cover his surprise and concentrated on chewing one of Gracie's coconut squares.

Gracie conceded the reporter's point. "However, as citizens, it's our duty to make sure our elected officials make the right decisions." Marybeth and Molly murmured their agreement.

"So," Mike continued in earnest, "you're saying that this petition is the *right* thing to do and that the council has made the *wrong* decision." He glanced at the others. "We've received a bunch of calls supporting the council, so right and wrong seem to be more a matter of opinion than any absolute determination."

"No surprise there!" someone said.

This seemed to trigger discussion. The noise level grew until it was impossible to hear what was being said. Finally, Susie Frantz called out in an authoritative voice. "Can we please be quiet!"

Silence fell. No one looked more surprised than Susie herself.

"Look, shouting won't get us anywhere," she went on, as though lecturing her own children. "I'd like to get home in half an hour or so. Is there any chance we could just let Gracie and Mike continue their conversation while the rest of us go through the list of volunteers?"

Mike Struthers looked at Gracie. "Did you mind my asking how you know you're in the right?"

Gracie sighed. Of course she understood that Willow Bend might not be in unanimous agreement. But it was well worth trying to find out what everyone did think. "Come on, Mike," Gracie said, "we're both veterans of the town wars."

He grinned and she continued, "And you know I'm not saying that our petition represents everybody's opinion. Not by a long shot. At least not yet. We'll simply see. If it is the case, then we feel it is acceptable to let the government know that they have made a decision that doesn't reflect the position of most of their constituents."

Mike said, "You're a marvel, Gracie! But even Rocky would never let me say it in print, despite the fact he totally agrees."

"Well, I'm not looking for personal approval here, even if I'm pleased to have it. Just write the article you think is fair to both sides."

He made a mock bow.

"And, just remember," she added, "even if He won't be signing the petition, the Lord *is* backing our side!"

This time he saluted.

Then they both shook hands and left the room.

11

GRACIE SPENT MUCH of Friday morning on the telephone, touching base with the team leaders and splitting the list of new volunteers as evenly as she could among them. Her only problem arose during a conversation with Cordelia Fountain. Gooseberry lay sleeping, curled on the top of the sofa until his eyes flickered open upon hearing Cordelia's piercing voice through the receiver.

"I won't have smokers in my tourist home!" she snapped into Gracie's ear. "I'm happy to have my volunteers congregate in the parlor, but no smoking! It's such a filthy habit and I don't allow my guests that liberty, so why would I grant it to others?"

"There's no reason to, Cordelia," Gracie soothed her. It would take a very foolish person, or possibly an extremely daring one, to light a cigarette on Cordelia Fountain's immaculate property. The large Victorian mansion was daunting enough, but one glare from the ramrod-straight proprietess usually reduced most people to a stunned and respectful silence. "I'm sure the canvassers will respect your wishes."

Now Cordelia suddenly shifted ground. "You know, Gracie? I was reviewing the names of my assigned volunteers and most have never even been here. It's actually a lovely opportunity, especially since word of mouth is the best advertising you can get. Tourist season's not far off, and though I know I always get busy—everyone who's been here does rave, of course!—making new contacts and showing off the house's splendid details can't ever hurt!"

"Of course! How clever you are!"

After wishing Cordelia well, Gracie dialed Rick at work and provided him with the necessary few corrections to the petition and sign-up sheet. He made the changes while they spoke and told her that she could swing by and pick up the final copies around lunch. Gracie was delighted, since she had already planned to drop by the businesses on Main Street and tell them about the petition. Now, she could furnish them with sign-up sheets and flyers.

She made a quick call to Kenneth Ebersole, who agreed to have the Waxmire Tabernacle's photocopier up and ready after lunch, then phoned Pat who wryly informed her that Eternal Hope's copying machine was champing at the bit, ready to do its ABC's. As the living room clock crept past noon, Gracie finally put down the receiver and, for the first time, noticed an enticing smell emanating from the kitchen.

"Soup's on," called Uncle Miltie.

"Coming!" Gracie tidied her papers and headed into the kitchen, where her uncle stood guard over a simmering saucepan. He motioned for her to sit. She turned to find her kitchen table divided into two: piles of envelopes and loose stamps filled one end, while two table settings were arranged and waiting at the other.

"Watch out for those piles," directed Uncle Miltie. "Paddy's part way through them."

Gracie nodded, and settled into a chair. "This is very nice. I'm starving and I forgot all about the time."

Uncle Miltie grinned, carried the saucepan over and slowly ladled out thick mushroom soup. After filling the pan with hot water, he returned with a plateful of ham and cheese sandwiches and joined her at the table. "Figured you had enough on your plate this morning, dear," he told her gruffly. "Dig in."

She reached across to squeeze his hand in thanks before hungrily biting into a sandwich.

"How are the arrangements coming?" Her uncle sipped a spoonful of soup.

Gracie swallowed, then replied, "Pretty well. It looks like we've got five to eight people on each team."

"Is that enough?"

Gracie shrugged. "I've no idea. We're just going to go out on Monday evening and see how far we get. Everyone's agreed to set aside Tuesday night, too, just in case. That is, except us choir stalwarts."

Her uncle reached for another sandwich. "Who's on your team?"

"Roy Bell, Lucille Murphy, Chuckie Moon and Quasi Weaver."

Uncle Miltie cocked his head. "*Hmm*, a cranky handyman, a chatty police dispatcher and two teenage boys with weird nicknames."

He finished his bowl of soup. "I don't know, Gracie, but I think you might need some more help. What are folks going to say when they catch sight of Chuckie's latest hair color or Quasi's pierced eyebrow?"

Gracie smiled. She knew he was teasing, as young Charles Moon was pretty much respectable these days, and was earnestly working on getting a college scholarship.

Her uncle now asked. "What would you say if Paddy and I threw our hats into the ring? He wasn't too keen when I first asked him, but he came around eventually. Of course, we're not as quick as the boys, nor as loud as the other two, but I'm confident we can help make a difference. Use the old charm, if common sense isn't good enough."

Keeping her face solemn, Gracie replied, "I'd *say* absolutely nothing ..."

Her uncle's face fell.

"Except this—" She stepped quickly to his side, and, throwing her arms around his neck, she bestowed a gentle kiss on his cheek. She beamed at him.

"You're a dear, Uncle Miltie."

The photocopier jammed again. As Gracie sighed and pulled up the cover, she wondered if the Waxmire Tabernacle machine was as ornery. She hoped not. Why is it, she thought, as she gently removed shredded bits of paper, that gadgets— ostensibly dreamed up to make our lives easier—seem to know when we're in a hurry? Exactly like a child, who suddenly forgets his glasses or his pocket money, just as his family is trying to rush out the door.

She glanced at her watch. It was 2:15 P.M. She was due to pick up the Waxmire copies in half an hour. She reset the machine, riffled the paper to remove moisture, crossed her fingers and reached for the start button. She had considered saying a prayer, but decided that requesting the Lord's intervention in this case was inappropriate. After all, He had better things to do with His time.

Gracie paused—Pat's instructions suddenly in her head— and remembered to give the machine a temporary time-out.

While she waited, she looked outside. From her spot on Eternal Hope's ground floor, she could see both approaches to the old wooden building. The sanctuary, chapel, main-floor bathroom and basement had been constructed over one hundred years ago. Gracie stood in the addition, which had been built in the seventies. This included a large Family Activity Center, more classrooms and a first-floor kitchen, which had been lovingly and gratefully designed by the women who used it the most.

The bulky figure of a warmly dressed postal carrier hurried along the main walkway past her window, his mittened hands pulling a small cart that bulged with mail bags. She thought of her uncle, whom she had left in the midst of examining a pile of stamps with a magnifying glass, and smiled. Perhaps he would find that first day cover or that three-cent plate block he kept talking about.

Another figure appeared, nimbly approaching the nearby side door. Although the man was dressed in an oversized jacket with the hood pulled up, Gracie immediately recognized his light step. Paddy O'Brien was entering the main floor. Perhaps the onetime clown was seeing Pastor Paul after all?

Pat Allen held the door open for him. As she turned, Gracie noticed that she was now wearing a colorful sweatshirt, a recent birthday gift from her sister Emily. Gracie could just make out the script that flowed across the cotton material: Peace of mind, Peace of heart, Peace of soul.

How suitable! Now, Gracie felt a brief prayer inspired by the sentiments displayed by Pat's sweatshirt most appropriate. *Dear Lord, please help Paddy to help himself in his troubling times. I know that he can find serenity and comfort in Your words if he'll only allow himself to ask for and listen to Your guidance. Direct Paul's words and actions so that Paddy can understand and embrace them, bringing peace to his heart, mind and soul. Amen.*

She punched the start button, and, with no further ado, perfect copies began spewing out with ease. She smiled and couldn't help herself from thanking God for what she felt was His timely intervention.

12

"HELLO, GRACIE!" Barry called out as she entered his barber shop. "Come on in! Is that the petition?"

Gracie nodded, then smiled a greeting at his two customers: Fred Bixler, half shaven and sitting in the main chair; and Harry Durant, seated nearby, critically examining his hairline in the large wall mirror. The small, but cheery shop was filled with the usual mixture of tonsorial odors: shampoo, hair spray and men's cologne.

"I'll sign that right away," said Barry, wiping his long razor before snapping it shut. He grabbed a pen and wrote his signature across the first line with a dramatic flourish, completed the address and phone number section, then he handed both pen and petition to the half-shaven man in front of him. "Here you go, Fred. Put your autograph right below mine."

Fred Bixler squinted at the sheet, then at Gracie. "So, what's this all about?"

Harry Durant stopped examining his hairline to pay attention.

"It's a petition to ask our town council to reconsider their recent decision to cut back library funding," Gracie replied, perching beside Harry.

She continued, "As a result of recent budget cuts, the library has chosen to stop purchasing audio books, among other things. I was asked by Anna and Joe Searfoss if I'd help them get the council to reconsider."

She handed each man one of the flyers. "Here."

Fred said, "Count me in. I can't tell you the number of times that Nancy's come home from her shift at the hospital and told me about some mystery or other she overheard a patient listening to."

He grinned and swiftly completed the petition. "Only problem is that most of the time, she never gets the chance to hear how it ended."

The threesome looked over to Harry. He finished reading the flyer, then studiously began combing his hair. Since he was nearly bald on top, this only took a few seconds. Aware of their stares, he slowly slicked down an errant curl, folded rough hands over his paunch then grunted. "Nothing personal, Gracie, but I'm not too keen on signing." He handed her the flyer. "So, if it's all the same to you guys, I won't."

His comment startled everyone. Then, after a long moment, they all replied at once.

"*Huh?*" exhaled Barry. "Of course, it's not all the same to us! For Pete's sakes, Harry, what have you got against audio books?"

Fred reared forward in the chair. "You're kidding, right?"

"Guys, please! Listen!" said Gracie, overcoming her surprise. "Harry is completely welcome to his opinion. I'm grateful he listened and read our material."

The other men still stared hard at their friend. He stubbornly met their gaze, then demanded, "What are you guys looking at? Gracie herself says it's all right if I don't sign. So there!"

"Well, you old coot!" Barry scolded him. "Would you at least tell us why not?"

"I'm surprised *you* of all folks don't know already," Harry retorted. "The taxes on my garage have gone up nearly thirty percent over the last five years. I don't know about you, Barry, but I'm happy to see the pain spread around some." He flushed slightly. "I'm sorry, Gracie. Anna and Joe are good people. I don't want them to suffer but fair is fair, and sometimes life isn't!"

Gracie nodded. "I understand, Harry. Thank you for your honesty."

Barry muttered under his breath, then flipped open his razor and began scraping Fred's cheek.

Gracie said good-bye and slipped out onto the street.

Shivering against the change in temperature, she hurried along the sidewalk toward Marge's gift shop. Harry hadn't been her first refusal. Earlier, she had experienced her first taste of opposition to the ABC petition in the Willow Mart. Although the owner of the local grocery store welcomed both flyer and petition, Gracie had been taken aback when a woman she barely knew had accosted her as she was taping a flyer to the front window.

"Hey, who do you think you are? I don't appreciate your cluttering up the window," the stranger had said.

"I'm sorry?"

She jabbed a long finger toward another flyer. "It's too close to mine."

Gracie peered at the pink and blue paper in question, an advertisement for a local day care center. "Well, Mrs. Hanley," replied Gracie, seeing the name on the bottom of the flyer, "I certainly didn't mean to obstruct anything." She unstuck her flyer and moved it an inch to the right, all the room she had, given the rest of the flyers tacked every which way onto the window. "How's that?"

At that moment, Mrs. Hanley had scowled. "Guess it'll do." Then she had sniffed and turned, but managed to toss another remark over her shoulder, "No one's going to sign that. I mean, who cares about audio books anyway?"

Now, Gracie yanked open Marge's shop door, relieved to be entering friendly territory.

Marge waved at her from the back. "You look like you could use a cup of coffee."

Gracie smiled at her best friend. "You read my mind. Any chance you could join me?"

"Sure. Give me a minute."

While she waited, Gracie placed the petition near the cash register, then added a small pile of flyers.

Marge returned, pulling on her coat. "You got them? Great." She held up a flyer and called to her part-time helper who was dusting shelves. "I'll be about half an hour. Would you mind sticking up one of these in the window?"

They were soon comfortably settled in a booth at Abe's. The deli was quiet, and they sipped their coffee gratefully in the cheerful room. Gracie idly read the specials of the day posted on the little board on the counter.

Moments later, Abe returned. He asked curiously, "How's it going?"

Gracie frowned slightly, thinking about Harry Durant.

"Something wrong with the coffee?" Abe asked, eyebrows raised in concern.

She quickly told him about her encounters with Harry Durant and Mrs. Hanley.

Marge chuckled. "Don't give them another thought. A lot of folks are on our side. You just wait and see. You can't expect everyone to agree with you, but most will."

Abe nodded emphatically. "I think you'll be pleasantly surprised at the number of names you'll get."

The deli's front door opened with a rush of cold wind. Paddy O'Brien stepped inside and mournfully glanced around. It was obvious from his expression that he wasn't sure of the reception he would get and worried about feeling out of place.

Gracie called out his name and waved.

Paddy appeared startled. Gracie called to him again, encouraging him to join them.

The only other customer glanced up from his paper and stared at the small man in the bulky coat. Paddy took a deep breath and walked to their booth, a wan smile on his wrinkled face. "Good afternoon, ladies," he said. He acknowledged Abe, who was now standing, with a slight nod.

"Hello, Paddy," replied Gracie. "Join us for a cup of coffee?"

Paddy looked doubtful.

Gracie noticed that the circles under his eyes had darkened and that his clothes now seemed overly large. She wondered if he had indeed met with Paul. It was hard to read his real mood. She wasn't sure how to bring it up without appearing as though she had been spying.

"I'm interrupting you...," he began, nervously.

"Nonsense!" Marge patted the booth beside her. "Come on, sit down. Please!"

Abe helped him remove his coat, took his order for tea and headed toward the counter. Paddy slipped in opposite Gracie. "How are you enjoying your stay so far?" said Gracie.

He answered in a flat tone. "You've got a nice town here. Nice people. But you know that, you don't need me to tell you."

Gracie replied honestly, "Willow Bend isn't to everyone's taste, since it is a small town, with all the virtues—and drawbacks—that entails."

Said Marge, "It may be small, but that doesn't stop me from stocking some of the same things you'd find in a shop in Chicago or San Francisco. I go to the big gift shows, and I try to pick the most unusual pieces of jewelry or ceramic. One little bank you might actually like, Paddy, is shaped like those little cars in the circus...."

Gracie was unable to kick her friend. Paddy was waiting for Marge to finish, a stricken expression on his face.

"You know," Marge continued, "the kind that seem to expand infinitely to contain dozens of ... clowns."

GRACIE WATCHED PADDY, whose shoulders now drooped. When he reached for his tea pot, Gracie noticed that his hand was shaking.

Gracie jumped in before Paddy could reply. "Marge, I'm quite sure Paddy doesn't need a bank, and maybe he's looking for things that don't, in fact, feature clowns when he's browsing around."

A grateful smile appeared on his face. Gracie continued, giving Les's cousin a chance to recover. "Did you know, Marge, that Uncle Miltie and Paddy have volunteered to collect signatures on my team?"

"On your team?" Marge seemed surprised. "Oh, I was going to ask Paddy to join my group. I'm with Phil, and we've got room for one more in his van." She sighed. "What a shame!"

Gracie raised an eyebrow.

"Will you look at the time?" Marge cried suddenly. "Sorry, you two, but I've got to get back!" Paddy slid out of the booth and assisted Marge in doing the same. They waved good-bye as Marge hurried out, still buttoning her long coat as she rushed past the front window.

"Can you sit for a few more minutes?" Paddy asked shyly.

Gracie nodded. She was done with the tasks she'd set herself and guessed that her uncle was still engrossed in his stamp search. He wouldn't stop until his stomach informed him that it was dinner time. That left a couple of hours yet.

Is he asking me to stay because he wants to talk, dear Lord? Should I let him take the lead or nudge him a bit? She decided to wait and see.

"Marge is a dear, isn't she?" Gracie felt she wanted to defend her friend just a bit. Then she changed the subject. "Any luck in the great stamp search?"

Paddy made a face. "Nothing so far and we've looked at hundreds." He paused, holding his rough hands out in front of him.

Gracie shifted, and tried to appear relaxed. *Perhaps, Lord, he only needs time to build up his courage. I sense You want me to just talk, and let him open up whenever he's ready.*

Sensing that Paddy's defenses were lowering, she added, "She didn't mean to upset you earlier, she just gets carried away sometimes."

He smiled thinly. "I know. It's not her fault, really. I'm just unable to talk about. . . ." He grimaced. "I suppose Les told you all about me. . . ."

Is this the time to push? Okay, Lord, I'm listening and hope I'm hearing You correctly. Gracie replied gently, "All he told me was that you were in some difficulty and could use a bit of luck and caring." She gave him a warm smile. "Not much different from anyone else, really. We all need help sometime. It's just harder for some to ask, that's all."

Paddy eyed her, then asked in a low tone, "Who do you turn to when you need help?"

"Well, the good Lord is with me, always." She met his gaze. "And with you, too."

Again, he hesitated before replying. "Perhaps. I haven't been able to hear Him lately."

"I'm sure He's there." Gracie took a breath, then plunged ahead. "I also find Paul Meyer to be a wise and sensitive counselor."

Paddy pursed his lips. "Aye. That's what Lester said."

"Have you considered speaking to him?"

He glanced over her shoulder to make sure they were not being overheard. "I actually went to see him this morning," he whispered. "Nice young chap but. . ."

Gracie kept her regard steady.

"I just couldn't do it. I know he's a kind, educated man. I

can see it in his face, but . . . somehow that makes it even harder." Paddy wearily rubbed his eyes. "I'm so tired, Gracie, sometimes I just can't think straight."

Gracie wanted to give him a hug. Instead, she just waited patiently.

After a while, he said hoarsely, "I miss the old life, Gracie. The big top, the animals, the people, my best mate—" He sighed. "I miss it all *so* much."

Pleased that he was opening up, even a little, Gracie gently prodded him on by asking, "Tell me about your life, Paddy. Please. It sounds so interesting to those of us who only pay admission to circuses."

Gracie suddenly caught a glimpse of the gap in Paddy's front teeth. Almost a smile, she thought.

"I don't know how interesting it was, but it's really the only life I've ever known" He looked directly at her. "Did Lester tell you that I joined the circus as a kid?"

Gracie nodded. "Every child's dream, but the difference is—you acted upon it."

This time, the smile was genuine. It dramatically changed the look of his face, softening the lines and lightening the shadows beneath his eyes. "Aye! When I look back at it, I shake my head. I must have been mad! Starkers! My poor mama." He looked sheepish. "Oh my, I broke her dear heart. But you know what's even crazier? I'd do it all over again, given half the chance. The Leaping Leprechaun, that's me."

Paddy paused, his expression turning rueful. "Would you listen to me? Rattling on about myself like this!"

Gracie held her breath, fearing that Paddy would again slip into silence.

"You were saying you'd run away all over again," Gracie now prompted him.

Paddy waited a moment before answering. The expression in his eyes seemed distant. Finally, he put down his cup and said, "That I would. It's been a grand life." He frowned slightly. "Well, almost."

After playing with his spoon for a moment, Paddy continued, "The mornings before a show are the best. There's a sense of anticipation and the air smells of popcorn, sawdust and face paint. Usually everyone's in a good mood, hoping for a sell-out. It's like we're one big family."

Gracie could almost hear the clamor, smell the melting butter and see the twisting and flipping of acrobats and jugglers.

The Irishman leaned forward, his eyes alight for the first time since Gracie had met him. "Have you ever seen a tiger stretch first thing in the morning, Gracie? His body seems as long as one of those old diesel trucks, and they make the same sound! A rumbling, deep in their throats!"

Gracie smiled and shook her head.

"Oh! You really should. It's a glorious sight." He blinked. "Well, I bet you have. Sort of."

She eyed him curiously. "I don't understand."

Paddy explained patiently. "I mean your own cat, Gooseberry. He probably goes through the same stretching routine every day."

Gracie laughed. "You're right! Although he sounds more like a startled bumblebee than a circus truck!"

"Aye, it was a grand life!" he repeated in a low tone.

Gracie watched the light die in his eyes and knew once again she had lost him. For a long time, neither said anything.

Finally, Paddy spoke. "Thank you for listening, dear lady." He lay several bills on the table and, dismissing Gracie's protests, rose. "It helps."

"I wish I could do more, Paddy. You only have to ask. There are people here who care about you. Not just Lester, Paul and me, but my uncle, Marge, even Rocky."

Paddy shrugged. "That one? No, thank you, Gracie, but I've never been too keen on newspaper folks. Seems getting the story's always more important than checking the facts." With that, he nodded and headed outside, leaving Gracie to wonder just what he meant by that last statement.

THE PARKING LOT of Keefer Memorial Hospital buzzed with traffic. This wasn't odd, given that Saturday afternoon was one of the busiest times for visitors. Exactly the reason Gracie, her uncle and Paddy O'Brien had decided to drop by. Phyllis Nickolson, who was on duty at the switchboard this morning, had agreed to display the petition sheets near the front entrance. Also, Nancy Bixler had offered to post flyers in the emergency and admitting windows before her mid-afternoon nursing shift.

But, even more importantly, Gracie had promised to visit Patsy Clayton. The young girl, crippled since birth, had undergone a series of serious operations that had not quenched her spirit nor her appetite for life. As her mother Marilyn had informed Gracie, this hospitalization was less painful but not necessarily less traumatic. Gracie learned that

Patsy was now having some tests to determine the results of her last reconstructive surgery.

Gracie had immediately offered to visit Patsy and had asked her uncle to accompany her, knowing that his corny jokes made the little girl giggle. Although slightly apprehensive about asking Paddy to come, too, she decided to risk it. After all, there was nothing like seeing an innocent child engulfed by a hospital bed to encourage you to count your own blessings.

Uncle Miltie looked at the stubborn snow drifts clinging to the brick exterior. "I don't much like going into hospitals, even as a visitor." As they paused for an ambulance to pull up, he glanced at his companions. "At my age, you just never know."

"Don't be silly, Uncle Miltie!" Gracie lightly scolded him. "You're as strong as an ox. Isn't he, Paddy?"

She glanced at Paddy's face. With a shock, she noticed that the wiry man's eyes were momentarily scrunched shut and that his face was as white as an orderly's coat. She tightened her grip on the little tin of shortbread she'd brought for Patsy. "Are you all right, Paddy?"

Her uncle said nothing.

Paddy looked around and made an obvious attempt to relax. "Of course," he replied stiffly. He rotated his shoulders, feigning soreness, then added, "Just a touch of arthritis. Catches me now and again." He moved forward with determination. "I'm fine, just fine."

Gracie and her uncle exchanged a puzzled look.

Gracie stopped to settle the business about the flyers and the petition, sending her uncle and Paddy on ahead to Patsy's room. As she approached the door, she heard her uncle's voice. She cautiously peered inside.

The first three beds she checked were empty. In the far corner near the window, four small children, two boys and two girls, were crowded onto the last bed, their eyes fixed on their two visitors. Parked to one side, a small wheelchair waited.

Uncle Miltie stood by the bed and in his hands, he held a hospital chart which he pretended to examine closely. Smiling, Gracie paused to listen. She heard her uncle clear his throat and ask in a very gruff voice, "Nurse O'Brien, could you tell me why there are 101 Dalmatians waiting in the outer office?"

Paddy squinted, then nodded emphatically. One of the children, a dark-haired boy, giggled. Patsy Clayton shushed him with her index finger.

Paddy replied, his voice now high-pitched. "Oh, it's such a sad and difficult case, Dr. Miltie. They all have the same troubles." He looked at the children, and sighed heavily. "Poor wee things, they keep seeing spots before their eyes!"

The youngsters burst into laughter.

"Just like me!" Patsy shouted, pointing to her pink polka-dot pajamas. The others clapped with delight.

"Mrs. Parks!" Patsy called, seeing Gracie in the doorway. She patted the bed. "Come and listen. Uncle Miltie's going to read us Tommy's story."

Gracie came in and gave her a hug. While the children happily munched on the shortbread, Patsy introduced them as Tommy, Max and Tracy. Max and Tracy jumped off the bed.

As Gracie said hello to them, she realized with a shock that the smaller boy, Tommy, was partially blind. His large brown eyes appeared unfocused when she spoke to him. Then, she remembered her pastor offering up a prayer of hope a couple of Sundays ago for the Hartzell family. He had added that their son, Thomas, was suffering from a rare eye disease, and was about to go into the hospital for another operation.

"No, no, not him," whispered Tommy. "The other one."

"Me?" Paddy asked.

Tommy's face brightened. "Yes."

"Please, Mr. O'Brien," said Patsy. "Tommy won't let us read it. And . . . well, he can't. His dad wrote it as a bedtime story just for him. Didn't he, Tommy?"

In reply, Tommy tapped the bed sheets until he found the pillow. Reaching underneath, he pulled out a few sheets of typewritten script, and held them out.

"Oh, I'm no good at storytelling, kid," Paddy said, pulling back. "I'm sure Uncle Miltie or Gracie would do a much better job."

The boy remained firm. "No. *You.*"

Paddy looked at Uncle Miltie and Gracie, but didn't make a move for the pages. Gracie couldn't understand what the problem was, but not wanting to disappoint the boy, she stepped in, and handed the story to Paddy. He didn't take it from her right away, but he didn't reject it, either.

For a moment, she berated herself for asking him along. Who did she think she was, bringing him to a place that she thought might be helpful to him? *Please, dear God,* she prayed. *Give him the strength and courage to get through this situation. Help him to not disappoint these dear children.*

The room became quiet. Everyone but Tommy was staring at Paddy.

The elderly man flushed, shook the pages for a moment then cleared his throat. "Okay, then. But don't say I didn't warn you." He inhaled, then began, "A long, long time ago, there . . . there lived a little farm boy named . . . Danny. He . . . *uh* . . . he was an only child and he had just one friend, a red and black rooster he called Doodle."

Gracie was watching Tommy's face and was taken aback to see the boy's expression open with surprise. She glanced at the other children. They were already caught up in the story.

"Now," continued Paddy, who slowly seemed to be warming to his task, "Ol' Doodle wasn't just *any* farmyard rooster. Not by a country mile. Nope. He had a bright yellow comb that flapped when he got excited—" Tracy giggled. ". . . and the sharpest, blackest eyes you ever did see." Paddy paused dramatically. "*Ahhh* . . . but that wasn't all, was it, children?"

Tommy smiled. "No," the young quartet happily sang out.

"You're absolutely right! Doodle was able to do something that no other rooster could do." Paddy dazzled the children with a gap-toothed smile. "Not only could he sing cock-a-doodle-doo, but, when he felt like it, he could speak to little Danny. In English. Perfect grammar, too."

"*Ohhh*," sighed Tracy. She pulled her doll close to her face.

Patsy leaned forward. "Wow."

The two boys grinned. Uncle Miltie's eyes twinkled.

Gracie settled into a nearby chair and became absorbed in the story, just like the children. As he went on, Paddy appeared more and more comfortable. Most importantly to Gracie, his eyes now gleamed with life.

Everyone in the room was engrossed with the Irishman's storytelling skills. No one noticed a man in a red parka waiting quietly at the door. When Paddy finally said the magic words, "And they lived happily ever after," the children's eyes were glistening.

Now that she knew what he was capable of, Gracie was more than ever determined to find a way to bring that sparkle permanently back into Paddy's green eyes.

The man in the red parka approached Gracie as they left the room. He introduced himself as Vic Hartzell, Tommy's father. "I can't thank you enough for cheering up my boy. He . . . he's a tough little guy; he's already been through this three times, but each time it failed. . . ." Eyes filling with tears, his voice trailed off.

He cleared his throat, took a breath and continued, "You . . . you see, they're operating for the fourth time. It will be the last one, whether or not it's successful. Tommy's got his hopes up so high. . . ."

Tommy must have heard his name for he called out, "Daddy?"

Vic Hartzell held a finger to his lips. "He doesn't know it's his last chance." Tommy shouted a second time. "I'd better go. Thank you again."

"Our prayers are with you," replied Gracie.

"Poor kid," whispered Gracie. Her companions nodded sadly.

As they strolled out into the wintry sunshine, everyone was silent.

"That was a fine story, Paddy," said Uncle Miltie, trying to shake the melancholy mood Vic Hartzell's news had left them in.

"I think you're being kind, is what I'd say," Paddy told Uncle Miltie. "If truth be told, it was nothing to crow about."

15

"THANK YOU ALL FOR COMING," said Pastor Paul Meyer as he stepped to the front of the altar at the end of the second Sunday service. "I've just got a couple of announcements before we leave today. First, I'd like to remind you that Easter is in just three weeks. So please, don't forget to circle Holy Thursday evening on your calendars. That's when we will be having our annual children's pageant."

"My second announcement is about something much more urgent." Paul glanced quickly up at the choir loft and caught Gracie's eye. She smiled in encouragement as he reached over to his pulpit to pick up a piece of paper. "I'm not sure if you're all aware of our efforts to ask the town council to review the cutbacks to the funding for audio books."

He spread out his arms, holding the paper high. "This is an

issue that affects many of our members—mostly the elderly and the infirm. And that makes the decision even crueler and much harder to accept. For some of these dear people, listening to audio books is the only joy they have in their lives. Most can't afford to buy them. Borrowing from the library is the only way."

He looked around at the congregation. "Fortunately, due to the organizing efforts of your friends and neighbors, a group has been formed to canvass our citizens, asking for their signatures in support. It's hoped that the powers-that-be might rethink their earlier decision and reinstate the funding."

He waved the paper. "This flyer—copies of which you'll find at the back—will give you more information. The canvassers will be out in force on Monday and Tuesday nights. You'll also find sign-up sheets in most of the local businesses along Main Street. Your support will be greatly appreciated. Of course, if you don't wish to sign, that's entirely within your rights. Oh, and just one more thing. Please remember to only sign once. We don't want to run into any problems resulting from duplicate signatures."

He then looked up at Barb Jennings. "Let us sing to and praise the Lord, and with the lifting of our combined voices may He understand how much we love and care for our neighbors, especially those less fortunate."

Barb took his cue and struck a note on the organ. The choir

began to sing. After a moment, the audience rose and joined in, sending a loud and mostly harmonious message up to the heavens.

At 9:13 P.M., Tuesday night, Chuckie Moon and Quasi Weaver dove into the back seat of Fannie Mae. "That's the last house on our list!" Chuckie crowed, eyes scanning a much-creased map of Willow Bend. He drew a large black check mark across their last street. "Okay, gang, ABC now stands for Already Been Checked!"

"Man, it's about time!" said Quasi, blowing on his hands. "My fingers are freezing."

The teenagers exchanged a high five with Uncle Miltie, who was in the front seat, then followed suit with Paddy as he slipped in beside them. Gracie then turned from the driver's seat with a smile. "Well done, gentlemen! We've completed our route. How many signatures tonight?"

Chuckie held up several crumpled sheets. "Almost as good as last night. Uncle Miltie and I collected nineteen."

Quasi laughed. "Is that all?" He glanced at Paddy, who pulled several crisp pages from a satchel he carried around his shoulder. Quasi flicked on a flashlight. Paddy quickly added up their results then said, "Young Quasi and I managed twenty-four, right?" Quasi nodded.

"With the fourteen I collected, we did pretty well," Gracie said.

A dented truck pulled alongside. Lucille Murphy rolled down the passenger window and called out a greeting.

"Why don't you two come back to our place for a cup of hot chocolate?" suggested Gracie.

Roy Bell tooted the horn in reply and gunned the engine.

In a few minutes, they were all in Gracie's living room, poring over the sign-up sheets waiting for the milk to heat. While pulling out the cocoa and mugs, Gracie had quickly listened to her messages, and was pleased to hear from both Molly Cook and Kenneth Ebersole. Both reported that their groups had finished and that they had provided Pat with the details.

Paddy stepped into the kitchen as she hung up, and offered to help.

"Thank you," said Gracie, handing him a plate of lemon squares and sugar cookies.

Instead of heading to join the others, Paddy hesitated.

"Is everything all right?" she asked, eyeing his thin face carefully. She thought he possibly had regained a little of his lost weight, but his expression remained guarded. "Quasi didn't cause you any trouble, did he?"

She had hoped that partnering Paddy with young Timothy Weaver would make it easier for the older man to canvass the houses of complete strangers. The teen was energetic, chatty and considerate, and from what Gracie had observed, appeared to get along well with everyone these days.

"Oh, no. No. He's a fine lad."

Paddy seemed to weigh something in his mind before continuing, "I only wanted to thank you, Gracie. You've helped me more than you know. I . . . I just wish there was some way to repay you."

Gracie opened her mouth. She was going to immediately respond that there was no need, when she realized that perhaps this might be Paddy's way of talking about his problems, maybe even asking for help.

Instead, she took a breath, and impulsively asked, "Do you want to talk about what happened to cause you to leave the circus?"

Paddy's mouth fell open. He looked simultaneously weary and belligerent. "Who told you about that? It's none of your business, or any one else's for that matter!"

Startled, Gracie blurted, "Lester did. But, honestly, he was simply trying to help!"

Paddy struggled to regain his composure. "I'm so sorry, Gracie, I shouldn't have snapped at you, of all people. Please, forgive me. It's . . . it's just that. . ." He hesitated. "Thank you for your concern." With that, he turned on his heel.

Chuckie was talking as Gracie reentered her living room a minute later. "Why were your numbers so low?" asked Chuckie. He looked genuinely curious.

Lucille shrugged. "Not our night. We kept running into

parents with young families who were afraid that if they signed, the town would target some of the children's summer programs."

Roy paused. Then he explained, "I started to tell them that if they both weren't working, it wouldn't be an issue." He motioned in the direction of Lucille, whose eyes widened in anticipation. "She told me not to. Said it would just upset them, and maybe even harden their position."

Uncle Miltie opened his mouth, then decided against commenting. Gooseberry trotted in and jumped into Quasi's lap. The boy smiled down at the big cat.

Gracie nodded. "I appreciate your point, Roy, but I think Lucille was right."

The phone rang.

"I'll get it." Uncle Miltie rose to pick up the receiver, while Gracie handed round the cocoa. "Hello, Cordelia. You folks finished yet?" He paused. "*Uh huh*. Who else have you heard from?" Another pause. "Good. *Hmm*, I think so. Just let me check with Gracie."

He held his hand over the receiver and asked, "We're supposed to phone our numbers into Pat at her house tonight, right?" Both teens nodded along with Gracie. "Then drop the actual petitions off at her church office sometime tomorrow?"

Gracie nodded.

Uncle Miltie repeated the instructions into the phone, then

hung up. He then said, "Looks like everyone's reported in except Phil."

"I guess that's not unexpected," commented Lucille, "given that he's got the longest route of any of us. . . ."

The telephone interrupted her.

"I'll get it," said Gracie.

Anna's voice immediately filled her ears. "Oh, Gracie, it's so exciting! We've just heard from Pat, who told us everyone's finished. And, guess what?"

"Yes, dear. What?"

The others watched Gracie with curiosity.

"You've done it! Pat said you've collected over five hundred signatures!"

Gracie agreed. "That it is."

"What'd she say?" Quasi hissed. "Yeah," added Chuckie. "Tell us!"

She waved them into silence. "Thank you, Anna. I'll tell my team the great news. And I'll call you tomorrow, all right?"

Chuckie jumped to his feet as she put down the receiver. "Come on, Mrs. Parks! Did we make it?"

"We certainly did."

"And that doesn't include the number of signatures on the sign-up sheets," Lucille added excitedly, "still waiting to be picked up at the local businesses and at the hospital!"

With his half-empty mug in hand, Uncle Miltie stood beside his niece. "To Gracie," he said, settling a quick kiss upon her cheek, "without whom none of this would have happened." He raised the mug.

"Right on!" added Chuckie.

They all clinked their mugs, smiling proudly at one another.

16

"SO PADDY ALREADY went through all those, right?" asked Gracie, pointing to a sloping pile of envelopes.

She and her uncle were seated at her kitchen table, but could barely see one another for the reference books, bags, shoe boxes and loose piles of paper. Gooseberry gazed down at them from his perch on the top of the refrigerator. His tail twitched every so often, like a friendly snake.

Gracie hadn't told her uncle about her brief but disturbing conversations with Paddy over the last few days. Since she hadn't really learned anything new, she wasn't sure what to say, so she decided to keep their little discussions to herself for the time being.

Uncle Miltie looked up from an overstuffed box and peered at his niece. "*Uh huh*. Not one stamp older than 1950. I think we can safely put them in the recycle bin."

He jerked a thumb toward a stuffed grocery bag that threatened to spill its dusty contents at any moment. "That bunch just came in from Molly. She found them shoved inside a closet. I guess she'll be looking for a new cleaning company."

Gracie paused, her nose tickling. She leaned back. "*Ahhh chooo!*"

Just as her uncle opened his mouth to bless her, a startled Gooseberry leapt from his lookout. He landed, nimbly enough, in the center of the table. Unfortunately, his back legs slipped on part of a plastic bag, panicking him further. Scrabbling for stability, he lunged across the cluttered surface, scattering stamps and envelopes in his wake.

"Hey! Stop!" shouted Uncle Miltie, reaching to catch him.

It was too late. The cat plopped onto the floor and streaked into the hallway, then bounded up the stairs.

Papers covered the kitchen floor. Holding her breath, Gracie looked across at her uncle. His face was growing redder by the minute.

"Look what that feline monster's done!"

Gracie held up a palm. "It was my fault, not Gooseberry's. I'm the one who sneezed."

He slumped back into his chair. "Oh! Just look at this mess!"

Gracie rose and bent down. "It's not so bad. Isn't this the pile that Paddy's already been through?"

Her uncle rose and examined the table. "I think so." He

moved to help his niece pick up the litter. He sighed, looking down at the disarray.

Staring at a heavily creased envelope, Gracie suddenly paused. "Didn't you say that Paddy hadn't found any stamps that were older than 1950?"

Uncle Miltie nodded. "Why?"

Gracie handed him the envelope. "Doesn't that look like 1946 to you?"

Her uncle grabbed his magnifying glass to confirm. "It sure does! How on earth did he miss that?"

Gracie continued to sort papers, tossing most into the recycle bin, but now she looked at every envelope. "There were a lot of stamps to go through. He probably just got tired."

Nodding, Uncle Miltie carefully put his new philatelic treasure on the kitchen counter. "Thank heavens you noticed!" he said. "It could be worth something."

"Don't thank me," replied Gracie, her eyes on the doorway. Gooseberry was there, quietly cleaning his back paws. "Thank him."

"*Hmmph!* Oh, all right. Gooseberry, old chum, thanks."

The cat ignored him and continued grooming himself.

Gracie grinned and reached to put the last few stamps into the bin. At the last moment, she pulled back her hand, her eye caught by an envelope with a partially torn stamp depicting the Statue of Liberty. "Uncle Miltie, didn't you say something, too, about 'First Day of Issue' being important?"

Her uncle's eyes narrowed. "Can be. Depends on the year, among other things. Why? You found one?"

She handed him her find.

Her uncle examined it carefully, then released a long, low whistle. "This is a first day cover of a 1954 Statue of Liberty three-cent stamp." His mouth split into a brilliant smile. Holding the envelope reverently between his thumb and forefinger, he added, "It's ripped a little but . . . I think it *could* be valuable, Gracie. Really valuable."

"Great!" she told him. "Just great!"

Her uncle barely noticed her reaction. "How on earth could Paddy have missed this one? That stamp from the forties, maybe. The year's a little blurry. But this!"

He held out the envelope. "Why, even I can read 'First Day of Issue' without using a magnifying glass." He settled back into his chair. "Gosh, Gracie, if you hadn't looked before you threw that stuff out, we'd never have found these."

He shook his head. "I thought I could trust Paddy to be careful, but I guess not." He hesitated for a moment. "You . . . you don't think he was planning to take these two himself at a later date, do you?"

"Of course I don't believe that. I'm sure Paddy wouldn't do anything of the sort. It's bound to be something innocent, Uncle Miltie, like his being tired or maybe even a little careless. And, no, I don't think there was any malice aforethought."

"I sure hope not," said her uncle. "I was beginning to think of him as a friend, but... now, I don't know what to think."

Gracie put the kettle on to boil. "Let's not make any hasty decisions, without finding out what Paddy has to say first, okay? I'm sure he's going to be just as surprised as you were. Probably a little embarrassed, too."

"Yeah. I guess so." Uncle Miltie shuffled a few envelopes, then added, "I'd sure feel mortified if I were in his shoes." He hesitated. "Poor guy. You know, he's having enough trouble as it is, isn't he? I surely don't want to add to his pain. Let's not tell him about his mistake, okay?"

"Okay," she replied softly. *Thank You, God, for helping my uncle to see past his own anger and find what truly matters: caring for others, especially in their hour of need.*

Suddenly, and joyfully, a passage from St. Mark entered her mind. "Amen I say to you, as long as you did it to one of these my least brethren, you did it to me."

"Your Audio Books Coalition petition should be on the program for our next meeting," said Ruth Stefano. The Willow Bend town council member lowered her voice. "I'm not supposed to tell you this, Gracie, but we've been expecting your call. I even held back on finalizing the agenda. Tell me, is it true, that you've obtained over five hundred signatures?"

Gracie shifted the phone to a more comfortable position. "Yes, Ruth," she proudly replied. "Nearly eight hundred, actually, at last count. Do you think it's a large enough number to get the council's attention?"

Ruth laughed lightly. "Oh, my yes. Don't worry about that, Gracie. You pretty well had our attention from day one. And good for you, I might add! I, for one, love seeing direct community involvement. It honestly makes my job as councilwoman more fulfilling."

Gracie paused. "I'm just not so sure my appreciation is shared by the rest of the council."

At that moment, Gracie's doorbell chimed. "You're saved by the bell," she told Ruth.

"I'm glad," Ruth replied. "Very glad. Because I couldn't ever speak for any of my fellow council members."

"Of course not," Gracie soothed her. "And I wouldn't have it any other way."

L ESTER TWOMLEY RUSHED ACROSS the threshold. "You've got to help me, Gracie!" he begged. "I'm really worried about Paddy! *Really* worried!"

"Oh, dear! Come in, Les," said Gracie. "Tell me what's wrong."

Her uncle poked his head out from the kitchen. "We'll both help, Lester. What's wrong?"

Gracie led the way into her kitchen. She sat him down, then poured him a cup of fresh coffee. Her uncle waited until Lester had taken a sip before asking his question again.

"It's going to sound a little crazy," Les said. "Maybe I'm overreacting. I don't know."

"It doesn't matter what you think it'll sound like, Les," Gracie reassured him. "Just tell us."

Les took a deep breath. "Okay. I just got a call from the

owner of my cousin's circus. Mister Nathaniel Dunn." He flushed slightly at the memory. "He didn't sound like a very nice man. Seems it took him a while to find me. Paddy didn't give him a forwarding address or even a phone number."

Les shook his head. "Anyway, he said that my cousin's mail is piling up—he'd forgotten to provide the post office with his new address—and now Dunn's threatening to throw it all into the trash if Paddy doesn't cover the costs of having it forwarded to my house."

Uncle Miltie shrugged. "That's not such a big deal, Les."

"I know, I know," replied Lester impatiently. "But he's not talking about the mail Paddy's received in the last few weeks." He looked between Gracie and her uncle. "Mr. Dunn told me that some of my cousin's mail is over six months old and has never been opened!"

"Never been opened," Gracie repeated. "That's odd."

Uncle Miltie snorted. "Well, I've heard of procrastinating, but this takes the cake."

Lester took a long breath. "And that's not all."

The others stared at him.

Les gulped again then nodded. Gracie refilled his cup. "Dunn claims he found a bunch of old, *opened* mail addressed to my cousin, in someone else's locker."

"Whose?" Gracie and her uncle both asked.

"A dead guy named Lawrie Agnew."

Uncle Miltie did a double take. "Did . . . did you say 'dead'?"

"Yep. For over six months."

Gracie was remembering her conversation with Paddy in Abe's Deli. The Irishman had mentioned having a best mate. "Paddy knew this man?"

Lester looked at Gracie. "Yeah. Dunn says they were the best of friends. For over fifty years. Agnew was also a clown. He had a routine with his wife until she passed away half a dozen or so years ago. After she died, Paddy and he combined their juggling acts."

"Well, no wonder your cousin is depressed!" Gracie folded her arms across her chest. "The poor man must be grieving for his friend."

Gracie sailed into the kitchen a week later, having just finished her morning walk. Kicking off her shoes, Gracie poured a glass of apple juice and sat sipping, relaxed, in her favorite chair. After the excitement of organizing the petition and undertaking the canvassing earlier in the month, Gracie had greatly appreciated the slower pace of the last few days.

She had invited Paddy O'Brien to dinner twice, but he had politely said no both times, giving no reason except that he felt a bit under the weather. Her uncle, who had managed to drag Paddy to play pinochle at the senior center once, told her he was now even more reticent than before. Gracie simply increased her prayers on his behalf and waited.

She knew from personal experience that time did indeed heal most wounds. Perhaps not completely, but at least to a point where the sufferer could take those very essential steps to move forward with his life. She also knew how comforting and beneficial it was to have someone to talk to during those dark months.

Gracie would be there, should Paddy call.

This overcast morning, after assisting Pat with some paperwork at the church, Gracie planned to shop for the ingredients necessary for Barb's anniversary party. The afternoon, Gracie had set aside for baking. The party was the next evening and Gracie always found that cakes were moister and tastier after a day "curing" in the refrigerator.

Her uncle strolled in and greeted her while wiping an errant bit of shaving cream off his neck. "So, back to the old busy, busy schedule, huh?" he commented, spying Gracie's "to do" list. He pulled out a box of cereal, then two bowls and next fished out a pair of spoons.

Gracie smiled and yanked open the refrigerator for the milk.

"It's not too bad," she said, pouring for both of them. "Mostly shopping and baking."

Uncle Miltie grunted while chewing. "Your idea of heaven, not mine."

Gracie waved her spoon in acknowledgment. "And you?"

"Haircut, then Paddy and I are also going shopping."

The spoon slipped from Gracie's fingers. "You're shopping! With Paddy! Whatever for?"

Her uncle's eyes twinkled slyly, and he placed a finger to his lips. "I'll never tell."

Two hours later, Gracie was still trying to guess what the two men might be buying while she pushed her shopping cart along the aisles of the Willow Mart.

"Hello, Mrs. Parks!" a girl's voice chirped.

Gracie turned and was delighted to see Patsy Clayton and her mother, Marilyn.

Patsy wheeled her chair alongside Gracie's cart. "Oh my, you've got a lot of stuff," commented the little girl. "Are you catering another party?"

Gracie smiled. "Yes, Patsy. And how are you?"

Marilyn nodded hello. "She's fine. The tests results were encouraging, weren't they, my love?"

Patsy wriggled in her chair, her small face beaming. "I don't have to go back for months and months, do I, Mama?"

Marilyn stroked her daughter's fine hair. "No, honey." She tugged at the wheelchair's handles. "Now, say good-bye. Your daddy's waiting and I'm sure Mrs. Parks is busy and hasn't got all day to spend chatting with us."

"Okay." Patsy waved at Gracie and spun her wheels so that the chair turned. "Oh, by the way," she said, twisting slightly to see Gracie. "Wasn't that a good fairy tale Mr. O'Brien told us?"

Gracie bent for a sack of flour, then nodded.

"I liked it much better than the one Tommy's dad wrote for him."

Since she was price-comparing two brands of chocolate cooking squares, it took Gracie a moment to register the girl's last comment. "*Huh? Uh*, wait a minute, Patsy," she called as the wheelchair disappeared around the end of the aisle.

A second later, the little girl rolled back into view. "Yes, Mrs. Parks?"

Gracie stepped toward her. "Did you say that you liked Mr. O'Brien's story *better* than the one written by Mr. Hartzell?"

Patsy nodded vehemently. "Much better."

Gracie hesitated, processing this information. "But . . . but I thought the fairy tale Tommy gave Mr. O'Brien *was* from Tommy's father."

By now, Marilyn was standing near her daughter, a puzzled look across her face.

"Yes," the girl said patiently, "it was. But it wasn't the story that Mr. O'Brien told us."

Astonished, Gracie managed to ask, "Are you sure?"

"Oh, yes. Tommy's dad wrote about a train." She stuck out her tongue. "Borrring!"

"But why didn't anyone say anything?"

Patsy shrugged. "Tracy and Max hadn't heard Mr. Hartzell's story yet. I was going to say something, but if Tommy was happy with it, then that was all right."

Gracie somehow managed to purchase the rest of the ingredients on her list, despite being mentally side-tracked by Patsy's startling revelation. Although impressed by Paddy O'Brien's creativity, she kept asking herself, "Why in the world would he make up a story rather than read one already there in front of him?"

⁂

"*Suurrprrizze!*"

A flashbulb popped. Gooseberry, who had been hiding under Gracie's coffee table, high-tailed it for the kitchen.

Barb Jennings blinked, momentarily slack-jawed in astonishment at the motley crowd assembled in Gracie's living room. "What's . . . what's going on?"

Paul Meyer, his face hidden by an old hockey mask, reached over to pull his black cape around the woman's shoulders. "Happy anniversary!" he shouted.

The others cheered.

Barb flushed. "Anniversary? What anniversary?" She looked around at her friends. "Why are you all dressed up?"

Marge Lawrence marched smartly forward. Clad in a crisp white skirt and blouse with blue piping, she halted beside Barb and snapped off a salute. Grinning, she handed Barb an envelope containing a greeting card, signed by the whole choir. "It's your tenth anniversary as our choir director. Happy anniversary!"

"*Hooray!*" the others joined in loudly.

"Why, thank you," Barb managed to say.

Paul led her toward the linen-covered table in the kitchen, which Marge had heaped high with confetti shaped like musical notes. Several trays of desserts jostled with plates of vegetables and dip. In the center rested a large rectangular chocolate cake, frosted by Gracie to resemble a piano keyboard.

Lester began twirling a baton festooned with streamers and strutted over to Barb. "We're all dressed like one of your favorite Broadway musicals," he said, punctuating each word with a spin. "Guess who I am, " added Les, tossing the baton into the air. He dropped it and blushed a deep crimson.

The others laughed.

Shaking her head in disbelief, Barb stared at his green and gold band leader's outfit. Marge chuckled. Suddenly, Barb's face lightened. *"The Music Man!"*

Lester grinned and successfully tossed the baton from one hand to the other.

"How about us?" called Rick Harding from the hallway as he and his wife jived toward them. Rick was sporting skin tight jeans, rolled up at the ankles and a white T-shirt, while Comfort looked stunning in a bright red dress that swirled when she walked. While Comfort curtseyed, Rick stood still, snapping his fingers at his side. Soon, all the men joined in and Gracie's living room echoed with staccato clicking.

Barb clapped her hands in delight. "Tony and Maria from *West Side Story!"*

The couple grinned, then executed a perfect spin and deep dip.

Everyone applauded.

Tears rushed into Barb's eyes. "Oh, my! It's too much!" Gracie offered her a tissue. "Oh, you're all so kind to me! I don't deserve—" Barb paused, staring at Gracie's little-girl dress and patent-leather shoes. Marge had helped Gracie to tease her curls so that her red hair twisted high on her head.

"*Annie*?" Barb asked, her face breaking into a broad smile.

Gracie smiled and hugged her friend. "Happy anniversary, Barb! The choir would be hopeless without you."

"You've got that right, partner," Don Delano drawled, sashaying up to Barb. He pushed back his cowboy hat with one thumb and hooked the other in his holster. "Thank you, ma'am. My word, ain't those corn plants elephant-eye high this year!"

Barb embraced him, saying, "Curly . . . *Oklahoma*!"

Nodding, Don grinned and doffed his hat.

Now Barb looked around the room, guessing the other musicals on display. "*South Pacific*!" Marge smiled. "*The Phantom of the Opera*!" Paul gave her a thumbs up.

Barb's knees nearly buckled when she saw Bert Benton stride forward with Tish Ball and Tyne Anderson dangling from either arm. The threesome looked like they were walking out of a 1950s movie set. Bert's hair was slicked back and the twins wore matching skirts, bobby socks and saddle shoes.

"*Grease!*" Barb managed to sputter. After a moment to collect herself, she asked, "This is so much fun! Whose idea was it?"

Several people pointed toward Gracie, while others called out her name.

Barb's face glowed as she squeezed her friend's hand. "I should have known," she whispered in Gracie's ear. "You're a wonder."

Gracie smiled at her. "Barb, we all owe you so much for what you bring to the choir and for what you give to us, as individuals and as an ensemble."

Now Marge approached Barb and presented her with a small gift-wrapped box. "Thank you, Barb, for your wonderful direction and friendship. This is a small token of the choir's appreciation."

Barb smiled and opened the box with a gasp of delight. Inside rested a gold grand piano, its cover open and embellished with a tiny clock face. She peered closely, then read the inscription aloud. "To our talented and patient friend, Barb Jennings, on the occasion of her tenth anniversary as the director of the Eternal Hope Community Church's choir. May . . . may . . ."

Her voice failed her.

Marge finished on her behalf. "May her baton continue to wave for many, many years."

Barb's face collapsed. The two women embraced, then the others moved forward, hugging their friend in turn.

"I...I don't know what to say," Barb eventually whispered. Her tear-stained face beamed with joy. "I'm just so grateful that you share my love of music and are a regular part of my life. Thank *you*." She held up her own glass and toasted her friends. "Here's to another ten years of singing the Lord's praises."

"Amen!" Bert called out.

"Now," continued Barb, "I'm sure everyone's itching to taste some of Gracie's wonderful food, so let's dig in!"

Many of the guests moved quickly into kitchen, and still chatting, began sampling in earnest. Gracie was just cutting into the cake's piano keys when the voices in the room suddenly faded. She looked up.

Two clowns had silently appeared.

THE CLOWNS WERE DRESSED nearly identically: white-greasepaint faces, rainbow wigs, red noses, baggy overalls and extra-large yellow shoes. One clown, however, sported a broad, upturned smile, but the painted mouth of the other curled down and deep red slashes marred his forhead. Each man held a large rubber ball, but the frowning clown wore a tall black hat.

Without a sound, the two bowed deeply and began tossing the balls back and forth. The audience shifted to give them room, noticing for the first time the small signs pinned to each man's back. The signs read: Who am I?

For the next few minutes, the two men performed an imaginative and entertaining routine whereby the clown without the hat, would distract his buddy by spinning, twirling or lobbing a ball and then attempt to knock the hat off the other's head. Once accomplished, the winning clown would doff his prize to the crowd, who cheered with delight. Every now and then, one clown would pretend to play a violin while the other danced a brief jig.

"Which one's Uncle Miltie?" asked Marge, moving to Gracie's side.

Gracie shook her head. Though she could easily distinguish her uncle's slower movements, she didn't want to spoil the magic. She started to admire how clearly and easily the two men were telling their jealous-of-the-other's-hat story, without ever uttering a single word.

That led her to think about something Paul had said several days earlier. At the time, she had tried to tell him that she believed the town council members would better understand the value of audio books if they had seen the women in the senior center happily listening to *Anne of Green Gables*.

Gracie's concentration was broken as Les pointed his baton at the smiling clown on his left and confidently announced, "You're my cousin Paddy!"

The clown hesitated, then shook his head slowly. His partner thrust out an arm, and the two quickly locked elbows and twirled. After a couple of spins, they stopped and waited.

It came back to her in a rush. Paul had declared that the council members needed to understand the need for audio books intuitively. Now, as Gracie watched the two clowns act out their pantomime, she *intuitively* understood their desire to own the black hat. She could have kissed the two old fools right there and then. She had an idea that might help the ABC cause!

"On the right," Don called. "Uncle Miltie for sure!"

This time, both clowns exchanged a look, then shook their wigs. Suddenly, a pumpkin-colored streak flashed through several legs and Gooseberry leapt into the arms of the clown on the left and began kneading at his costume.

"Uncle Miltie!" everyone cried.

The happy clown held up the big cat and pretended to shake it with displeasure.

Once both men had yanked off their wigs and noses, identification was easy. Although she had already guessed, Gracie still felt sad to see that Paddy had played the part of the gloomy clown.

"Had you going, didn't we?" said Uncle Miltie with a grin big enough to match his makeup. He and Paddy O'Brien shook hands.

"Hey, guys," offered Don, "that was a great routine."

"Wonderful," added Barb. "Thank you."

Uncle Miltie straightened his red nose and asked, "Can you guess which musical we represented?"

Barb hesitated. Suddenly, her face widened with a smile. "Of course! 'Send in the Clowns' from *A Little Night Music*."

Uncle Miltie added, "We're mighty glad we could make you laugh." Paddy nodded.

Les moved forward. "Everyone, this is my dear cousin, Paddy." He reached out. "If you haven't already met him, why don't you come say hi now."

"So, what did you think?" Uncle Miltie looked expectant.

Gracie eyed her uncle. Even though his hairline was damp and his make-up ran down his cheeks, his blue eyes sparkled. "You two were great. Just great."

"Could you really tell us apart? I mean before old Gooseberry spoiled it?"

Gracie glanced at Marge. "It wasn't easy, but since I live with you I figured it out."

"Not me," Marge said.

"Really?" Uncle Miltie beamed. "We weren't half bad, were we?"

"How did you get Paddy to dress up?" asked Gracie.

Her uncle looked exceedingly pleased with himself. "I mentioned having to find something to wear to this party, then I told him that I'd always wanted to be a clown and nothing would make me happier than to learn from the best. It took some convincing, I confess." He winked happily. "But flattery works every time."

"So that's what you two were doing when you said you were going shopping!"

Uncle Miltie tweaked his red nose in answer.

Paul approached, holding two glasses of punch. He gave one to each of the ladies, then offered to return and fill one for Uncle Miltie.

The older man thanked him but declined. "I'll get my own," he insisted.

"He's just marvelous," said Paul, as they watched Uncle Miltie make a beeline for the food table. Soon, he was joined by Paddy.

"I know," replied Gracie softly, watching her uncle.

Marge now asked her friend, "Were you as surprised as the rest of us?"

Gracie nodded. "All I knew was that they were going shopping. Never in a million years would I have imagined that it was for wigs and makeup!"

Marybeth Bower approached. "Hi, Gracie, I've been meaning to ask—is everything all set for the town council meeting?"

Gracie nodded. "Yep. All set." She glanced at her friends. "I got an idea while watching Paddy and Uncle Miltie's routine, though."

Paul's eyebrows shot up.

"What sort of idea?" asked Marge.

"Well, it really stems from something Paul said to me a few days ago."

The other women regarded Paul with anticipation.

He shrugged. "Sorry, ladies. I don't know what Gracie's referring to. Exactly which conversation do you mean, Gracie?"

Gracie explained, "You see, when I watched Uncle Miltie and Paddy go through their mime routine, it hit me!"

Marybeth was intrigued. "What hit you?"

"We in the audience knew instinctively that each clown wanted the black hat. Instead of telling us about it, the men *showed* us."

"Gosh, you're absolutely right!" exclaimed Marge. "You know, I really did understand exactly what they were doing, I almost forgot that they weren't talking!"

Paul and Marybeth nodded in agreement.

Paul added, "It was as clear as if they were shouting it at the top of their lungs."

"Exactly!" replied Gracie. "Well, what if we were able to demonstrate, to show, to the town council what it feels like to really need audio books? Not to just enjoy them every now and again, but to depend on them."

The others were silent for several seconds.

Marybeth frowned. "I'm not sure I understand, Gracie. You mean, somehow get this idea across without telling the council members in words?"

"Yes, Marybeth. It may sound strange, but I believe it would be a much more powerful message if our council members really understood, even if only for just a few moments, what it's like to be someone like Anna Searfoss. If we could help them experience life from Anna's perspective, they might appreciate why she and others like her rely so heavily on audio books."

Marybeth's expression remained puzzled.

"Like walking a mile in another person's shoes?" Marge offered tentatively.

"Exactly the idea! Thank you, Marge," replied Gracie. "That's just what we have to do."

Paul stroked his chin. "*Hmm*, getting them to experience another person's perspective. I like it, Gracie. But how are we going to go about it?"

"Well, I haven't had much time to think about it, but I have an idea. Let me run it by you now...."

With Marybeth and Paul nodding their approval, Gracie explained her notion as clearly as she could.

As soon as she was done, Marybeth exclaimed, "I love it, Gracie! But it's a bit unusual, to say the least. Do you think they'll let us do it?"

"I don't know," replied Gracie. "But if you guys think it's worth exploring, I'd be willing to test it out, say on one member, and see what reaction I get."

"I'm all for it," Paul said. "Any idea which member might be your best bet?"

"Ann O'Neill," offered Marge.

Marybeth shook her head. "Ann's a nice woman, but she's a lawyer, and I don't see a lawyer being open enough to something as new as this."

Gracie agreed. "I was thinking about Ruth Stefano."

"Perfect!" declared Paul.

A few minutes later, Gracie was refilling her glass at the food table. Her uncle sidled up to her, grabbed a cookie and handed it to her. He then looked around the room, eyes settling on their guest of honor. "Did she like the piano?"

Gracie replied, "Just look at her." Barb Jennings was leaning against the kitchen table, talking to Paddy, Paul and Estelle. "She hasn't let it out of her sight since she got it."

Just then, Barb handed the gift to Paddy, saying, "You've just got to read the inscription. I'm so lucky to have these people as friends."

Paddy awkwardly turned the piano in his hands for a long moment. He squinted at the engraving momentarily, then muttered, "*Uh*, I'm sorry, but I've forgotten my glasses." He handed it back, asking, "Would you do me the honor?"

While Gracie watched, Barb smiled and recited the inscription from heart. Something about the moment seemed odd, but Gracie was at a loss to say why.

"Why, that's brilliant," Paddy was saying. "Just brilliant."

"How's the stamp collecting?" asked Lester, wandering over. "My cousin says you've struck out so far."

"Well, not exactly," replied Uncle Miltie. "Gracie herself found two possibly valuable stamps."

Paddy must have overheard, because he turned to them

with a puzzled expression. "I thought we hadn't discovered anything of merit."

Uncle Miltie shook his head. "We didn't, Gracie did."

Gracie barely heard him, as she kept trying to remember what had just struck her as so unusual.

"I'm sorry," Uncle Miltie continued apologetically to Paddy. "In all the excitement, I clean forgot to tell you."

"Gracie found them? You must have received some new ones, then?"

Uncle Miltie hesitated. "*Uh . . .* yeah."

Paddy turned to Gracie. "Well, done, my dear!"

Still distracted, Gracie didn't reply.

"Gracie?" Paddy repeated. "Is there anything wrong?"

She blinked. "Oh, I'm sorry, Paddy! What did you say?"

He repeated his question.

"Oh, no, no, of course, there's nothing wrong."

But there was. Gracie was certain of it. She was also certain that she had missed observing something in the last few minutes that might have given her an insight into Paddy's problem. However, there was no time to ponder. There was food to be restocked, glasses to be refilled and guests to be entertained.

Plenty of time to worry about the unhappy clown later. Right now, the most important smile was her own.

19

"I'M NOT SURE WE EVEN NEED to have your group make a formal presentation," Ruth Stefano said.

Gracie leaned forward in her kitchen chair. "Oh, really?" When Gracie had called the councilwoman to confirm her group's spot on the agenda for the council's next meeting, she certainly hadn't expected this response.

Uncle Miltie hesitated in the middle of making a BLT to listen.

"Well, I've got to admit that when Pat Allen submitted your brief and the pages of signatures on Monday," Ruth continued, "it really got the council's attention. No one at the town hall can remember ever receiving that much feedback on any issue. Of course, it doesn't make our job any easier."

She took a breath. "I think we have everything we need for our review."

"Perhaps you do," replied Gracie, "but I was hoping you would indulge me for a moment."

"Indulge you?"

"Yes. Our coalition is pleased that you recognize the extent of our support base. However, we were hoping to introduce some more evidence."

"More evidence? You've collected more signatures?"

"No, not that, Ruth. May I run an idea by you, before making a formal request to the council?"

Ruth paused.

Gracie rushed to add, "Please realize, Ruth, that I'm not going to put you in an improper position. It's really just that I'd like to get your opinion on something. If you feel my idea isn't worth going ahead on, then I'll forget it and I won't waste the council's time."

At the quick change in his niece's tone, Uncle Miltie stopped in mid-chew and swallowed hard.

"Oh. Well, *that* sounds all right," Ruth responded. "What do you have in mind?"

Inhaling deeply, Gracie put her idea to the councilwoman.

When she had finished, Ruth Stefano took a long time in replying. Finally, she said, "It's a very unusual suggestion, Gracie. Quiet remarkable. I can't guarantee that all the members will be in favor, but I like what you're trying to accomplish."

Gracie sighed in relief. "Thank you, Ruth! May I ask how you'd suggest I approach the council?"

"Why don't you let me touch base with them? Your group is already slated for our next meeting, so nothing really needs to be done."

"I . . . I was hoping—"

Ruth interrupted Gracie's comment. "Don't worry. I won't reveal exactly what you're going to do. I'll just let my fellow councilors know that your presentation will be . . . *uh*, shall we say . . . an unorthodox demonstration? Is that acceptable?"

"Perfect." Gracie was delighted with the councilwoman's positive reaction. "Thank you, Ruth."

"Don't thank me just yet, Gracie," came Ruth's dry reply.

Gracie paused, her heart sinking. "Why not?"

"Well, for one thing, even if your little strategy works, we still don't know how we can find the money to give the library."

Gracie replied, as positively as she dared, "Oh, Ruth, I'm sure you can find a way. Don't forget, there are many people in Willow Bend who are interested and willing to help out. In any way they can."

Ruth sighed into the receiver. "Well, Gracie, I'm very glad to hear you say that. Now, I have something to ask of you."

"Yes?"

"Well, as you know, I support your coalition and the need to return those funds to the library. I have learned, in my years as a council member, that it's always best at our meetings to be prepared to strike quickly, if and when the chance arrives. Often, if you're not ready to put an alternative idea forward, your opportunity may be lost forever."

Wondering where she was heading, Gracie squeezed the receiver more tightly.

"So, if all goes well at the meeting," Ruth continued, "I would like to suggest the formation of a new committee."

Gracie's grip relaxed. She hoped she knew where Ruth was headed, but asked, just to be sure. "Why are you telling me?"

She crossed her fingers and waited.

"Because my plan is to have the council members and voting citizens together on this committee. I'd like to give them a mandate to review all the planned cutbacks and then attempt to come up with more acceptable solutions." Ruth hesitated again. "Now, I know you've already done so much, Gracie, but would you at least consider being involved?"

"I don't need to."

"Oh, dear," replied Ruth, her voice suddenly low. She stopped speaking, apparently at a loss for words.

Gracie smiled into the receiver. "I'm sorry, Ruth, but I think you've misunderstood. I don't need to *consider* your request. I'd love to volunteer."

Her uncle looked up from his lunch. "Sounds like you're going to be spending some time over at the town hall." He flashed a smile. "Well done, my girl! If anyone can help Willow Bend find a way to subsidize Anna's audio books, you can."

Well, dear Lord, I guess You've finally shown me the way, haven't You? Thank You for also giving me the will. I promise to do my best to help our town make decisions that will benefit everyone."

ANNA SEARFOSS LEANED BACK in her kitchen chair listening to Gracie. Then she clapped her hands lightly and said, "Oh, Gracie, I can't wait to go to the library tomorrow! I'm going to reorder all my audio books." She turned slightly toward her husband, who was reaching for a knife to cut Gracie's gift of a freshly baked banana-nut loaf. "We still have the list, don't we, Joe?"

Joe frowned. "I bet it's somewhere, dear." Anna's face fell. "And if not," he added quickly, "I know that Mary will still have it on her computer."

"She will?"

"I'm sure Joe's right," added Gracie, catching Joe's worried look. "Your request will still be in the system." Gracie crossed her fingers under the table.

Anna said, "Oh, that's good." She sipped her tea.

After seeing how desperately the elderly woman needed her audio books, Gracie didn't like what she had to tell Anna, but she wanted to try and prepare her friend for the worst.

"Now, Anna," Gracie began gently, leaning forward in her chair, "you've got to remember that what I've just told you about the committee doesn't mean that the funding for the library's audio book collection will automatically be reinstated."

Joe turned from cutting the loaf to ask, "But, surely, they wouldn't ask you to present your petition if they weren't going to change their previous decision?" He handed his wife a plate with a thick slice. Gracie was always touched to see how her friend made sure his nearly blind wife knew exactly where the plate was.

The pair coped well. Once a week, someone from Eternal Hope dropped by to bring a meal or two and to give Joe and Anna a hand in tackling the myriad of domestic chores necessary, allowing the couple to remain in their beloved bungalow.

While Anna thanked her husband for the treat, Gracie rose and refilled their mugs with tea.

"I honestly don't know, Joe," replied Gracie. "Just because they're willing to look at all the signatures we've obtained and let us present our case, doesn't mean they can or will reverse their decision."

He looked so discouraged that Gracie added, "What I *do*

know, is that the council members are willing to recognize our opposition and wants to see what can be done. That doesn't necessarily mean that they will find more money. I just think you both should be prepared in case the committee makes the same recommendation and the cuts to the library stand."

Anna protested, "Then all your work and all those signatures that you and so many others collected will have been for naught. Oh, dear, I hope not!"

Joe didn't say anything, but he let his shoulders sag.

"So do I," replied Gracie, wishing with all her heart that she could tell her friend not to worry—and that on her next visit to the Willow Bend library, her cherished audio books would be waiting. "I promise you both to do my very best to make sure that doesn't happen."

Anna smiled. "I know you will, Gracie. You've already done so much, my dear, I hate to think you have to do any more."

Joe nodded his appreciation. "We're so grateful to you, Gracie, in so many ways. But don't you worry about us. Right, Anna?"

He looked at his wife affectionately. "We've weathered many a storm in our lives and, somehow we've always managed to survive. Haven't we, my gal?" He reached over to gently squeeze Anna's shoulders.

She patted his hand.

"Just promise me one thing, Gracie."

Gracie gave him her full attention.

"Just tell those people on the committee that folks may doubt what they say, but they'll believe what they do."

She was happy to be reminded of the fact. "I'll tell them, Joe. Thanks."

Little shivers of panic started as Gracie steered Fannie Mae through the town's slushy streets. Just because she had an idea for a dramatic way to catch the council members' attention didn't necessarily mean much. After all, what did she know about the challenges and constraints involved in municipal cutbacks, civic funding priorities or appeasing a constituency?

She waited at a stop light, thinking. She had watched Elmo at work as mayor, but that was then and this was now.

So, other than her demonstration idea, what else could she possibly offer the town committee? All she knew was that many residents would be disappointed, some even devastated, if the library's funds were not reinstated. That part was easy. How to reorient the budget reductions or to seek other sources of money, was the real challenge.

Oh, El, she thought, what would you do in this situation? The light changed and she pressed on the accelerator pedal. As she drove along, Gracie tried to remember what the budget meetings had been like when her husband was mayor. She had often attended, even volunteering to take notes on occasion.

It took several blocks, but finally she recalled one instance, early in Elmo's first term when he was still feeling his way into the job, when a pair of council members were asking the town to support two new initiatives.

Elmo had immediately reminded the council that there were sufficient funds for only one initiative. He then provided each member with the same opportunity to put forward their case, as well as giving the others time to ask questions. After some further discussion, Elmo managed to get one member to admit that his initiative could be launched in two phases, although it clearly wasn't the favored stance.

In the end, the members were evenly split and Elmo was forced to cast the critical vote. He did so, after some reflection, and his decision to partially fund both initiatives surprised many, and angered more than one.

That evening on the way home, El had revealed to his wife how uneasy and insecure he'd been as he made the final decision.

Gracie had been surprised. "But why?" she had asked him. "It seems to me that not only did you do the right thing, you did something that the others hadn't even thought of."

"Finding new solutions to old problems is what's needed, I know. But as I'm learning the in's and out's of this job, dear, I'm beginning to appreciate more and more how important it is to work *with* the council."

Gracie shrugged. "Maybe so, but sometimes, that's not always possible."

He'd drummed his fingers on the steering wheel. "True. It's just that I think I could have been more tactful and let some of the others suggest the two-phased funding option." He sighed. "I fear I've made an enemy or two tonight, and that might haunt me in the future. I really wish I was more experienced."

At the time, Gracie had allayed his fears, by replying, "My dear Mr. Mayor, you know better than most that you can't please everyone. Working with those council members is no different than working with the members of our church board. And you've done that for years! All you can do is be honest, give your best and never give up."

He had smiled at her, and said, "You're absolutely right, Mrs. Parks."

The memory of his brilliant smile almost made Gracie weep, but as she stopped the car, she paused. Why, she thought, I've also been attending church meetings and participating in budget decisions for years!

She rested against the seat and raised her eyes skyward. Thank you, dear, for letting me know that I *do* have the experience. And I'll remember your comment and try to involve as many people in the solution we arrive at as I possibly can.

I'M GREATLY BEHOLDEN to you, Gracie," Paddy O'Brien said, "for coming along and bringing treats for the kiddies." He twisted in Fannie Mae's front seat to address Uncle Miltie who was in the back, once again dressed as a cheerful clown. "And to you, my friend. Without you, I don't think I'd ever have put on a wig or face paint again."

In salute, Uncle Miltie tapped his own red nose smartly.

"We're both delighted to join you, Paddy. Little Tommy's going to be very surprised to have two clowns visit him!"

She somehow hadn't seen Paddy since Barb's party. Although he still seemed like he was functioning with only half his heart, Gracie was pleased that he was making this effort to help Tommy. She had considered questioning the older man as to why he made up a story before, rather than read the one originally written for Tommy, but had decided against it.

What would she gain? Paddy was bound to feel threatened, possibly challenged. And for what? To satisfy her own inappropriate curiosity? No, whatever the reason, Gracie didn't feel it was important enough to risk adding more misfortune to the man's current woes.

"I sure hope so," replied Paddy. "Poor wee lad, going under the knife in a couple of days. I'm not even sure how much he can see but, just in case...." He glanced at his make-up in the rear view mirror. Apparently satisfied with the huge smile and oval eyes that greeted him there, he ordered, "Okay, let's go make the little guy laugh!"

Gracie grinned as she watched the faces of passersby—first shocked, then delighted—as the two gaudily dressed men emerged from her car and stuffed their wigs on top of their heads.

They linked arms and marched through the wide doors of Keefer Memorial Hospital.

Tommy was alone, lying very still. Gracie's heart did a few flip-flops when she saw how defenseless he looked. She glanced around. The three empty beds were made up and ready for their new occupants, who, Gracie guessed, would arrive later that afternoon.

"*Yooo hooo!*" Paddy sang out. "Is there anyone in here named Tony, Teddy, Timm—no, no, no. I've got that wrong. It's Tommy! Master Thomas Hartzell, of course, it is."

The little boy cocked his head and squinted in their direction. "Mr...*uh*...Mr. O'Brien, is that you?"

"Sure it is, laddie," Paddy called, tramping into the room. "I've brought your old pal, Dr. Miltie, and Mrs. Parks. We've come to say hello."

Tommy smiled faintly. "What's that on your face? Come closer."

"Why don't you tell me?" replied Paddy, moving near enough so that boy could reach out and touch him.

The boy's hands tentatively reached upwards. When he fingered Paddy's nose, Paddy said, "Go on, lad. Give it a squeeze."

Tommy smiled and pinched softly.

Simultaneously, Paddy squeezed a small horn, hidden in his pocket.

Tommy shrieked with joy, then pinched harder.

The horn blasted louder.

The twosome then played the pinch, squeeze and honk routine for a couple of minutes, while Gracie and Uncle Miltie watched with delight.

"Now, why don't you give Dr. Miltie's hair a bit of a tug," Paddy suggested.

Uncle Miltie stepped up. When the boy's fingers touched his wig, Uncle Miltie blew into a small whistle. The more Tommy yanked, the higher the toot. After several tugs,

Tommy just squinted hard at the two men, as though trying to take it all in. "You're silly!" he pronounced finally, giggling.

Paddy danced a little jig, then responded, "Hey, who're you calling silly?"

"Yeah," added Uncle Miltie, pretending to bump into Paddy.

Tommy clapped. "Would you read me another story, Mr. O'Brien?" Before Paddy could respond, he had tugged out a children's book from underneath his sheet and shoved it into Paddy's hands.

"Oh, my, isn't this a clever little book!" crooned Paddy. He admired the cover for a long time. "Hey, wait a minute!" He honked his little horn. "I've got an idea. Yes, indeedy. Why don't we ask Dr. Miltie to read the story while I act it out? How would you like that, my boy?"

Paddy passed the book to Uncle Miltie, who settled onto one of the empty beds. Gracie slipped down beside him. Then, in a deep voice, Uncle Miltie began reading the tale of a very little knight and a very large giant.

Gracie enjoyed the performance almost as much as Tommy. Paddy was an exceptional mime and tirelessly inventive with props. At one point, playing the part of the young knight, he flung a sheet round his shoulders and straddled a bench. Leaning forward, while hoisting a mop as if it were a lance, he seemed to be rushing out to defend his homeland against the flame-breathing giant.

When Uncle Miltie finally closed the book, the small boy started to cry. Paddy rushed to his bedside, whispering gentle words of encouragement. After a while, Tommy's eyelids became heavy. Just before he fell asleep, he reached up to squeeze Paddy's nose one more time. "You're my hero," he whispered, eyes fluttering. "I've never seen a circus clown up close before."

Tenderly stroking his forehead until he fell asleep, Paddy told him, "You're the real hero, little man. Good night and God bless."

I'M SORRY THEY'RE NOT WORTH very much," Gracie said, taking her eyes off the road to glance at her uncle. He was slumped in Fannie Mae's passenger seat, staring dejectedly down the quiet highway that linked Willow Bend to Mason City. A few cows were sniffing the yellowish winter stubble in a nearby field as they sped by.

Uncle Miltie held up his hands in defeat. "It's not your fault, Gracie. After all, you're the one who found them. We would never even have made this trip to Mason City, and I've wanted to visit that stamp store for ages." He examined the package of stamps on his lap for the tenth time. "It's just that I was hoping for more. I figured that the rip was going to be a problem, but who would have known that color was so important?"

Gracie nodded sympathetically. "That really surprised me.

It's a shame the Statue of Liberty stamp had faded so badly." She checked her speed, then continued, "Well, at least two of the stamps are worth something."

Her uncle snorted. "A lousy eight dollars."

Gracie raised her eyebrows. "Not bad for something with a face value of three cents."

Uncle Miltie looked again at the stamps. "Yeah, I guess you're right, but it sure isn't going to go far in covering the costs for new audio books."

Gracie did a double take. "New audio books!"

Her uncle flushed slightly. "Yeah. I thought maybe I could raise some money for the library. Just in case your committee can't come to some agreement." He thrust out his jaw. "I hate to think Anna won't be listening to her favorite stories."

Gracie wanted to reach across and hug him, but wisely kept her hands on the wheel, instead exclaiming, "Why, Uncle Miltie! That's one of the sweetest ideas you've had in a long time! Anna will be so touched."

Slightly embarrassed by her reaction, he replied gruffly, "Well, unless I hit the jackpot, there's no need to tell her."

"I don't know about that," Gracie replied. "I think she and Joe will be amazed that you could even get eight dollars for a pair of old stamps."

A grin slowly spread across his face. "That *is* a pretty good return, isn't it?"

Gracie smiled. She could see the wheels turning inside his

mind. She turned off the highway and onto the road that led into Willow Bend. Most of the snow had melted. Only small mounds around the electrical poles and the occasional obstinate drift remained. Soon, she thought, the new shoots will blanket the ground, and bright green buds will pop out on the now-barren trees.

Her uncle suddenly leaned forward, fingers bouncing on his knee. "I can't wait to get home, Gracie! Ken Ebersole called yesterday to tell me they've got all kinds of old letters stashed away in Waxmire's attic. He's agreed to let me have them if I offer to share any profits with the Tabernacle."

He leaned against the window, staring at the horizon. "You just never know. One of those letters might carry the famous inverted airplane stamp."

Gracie pulled away from a stop sign. "The famous what?"

"Remember when the philatelic guy was telling us some of the errors that have occurred during the printing of stamps?"

She didn't really remember any details as she had let her mind wander when the two men started talking, but she nodded anyway.

"Well, one of the most well-known errors happened on a twenty-four-cent U.S. stamp in 1918. The airplane was accidentally printed upside down. Only one hundred of the misprinted stamps were found, and today, mint ones fetch over one-hundred and fifty thousand dollars!" He opened and closed his mouth in astonishment. "Imagine how many audio books that would buy!"

They didn't have time to fantasize any further. As Gracie pulled into the driveway, Lester Twomley was skipping down her front steps to meet them. Tucked under his arm was an envelope, bursting at the seams.

"Most of these are from Social Security!" Uncle Miltie exclaimed several minutes later as the threesome sat around Gracie's kitchen table, waiting for the coffee to percolate. He thrust a fistful of unopened letters into the air.

Lester nodded. "I know. That's what really got me worried. When Dunn, the circus owner called about Paddy's mail, I never imagined there'd be this much!"

Gracie reached across to examine a sealed envelope from the Social Security Administration. "Why here's a letter dated over four months ago!"

Uncle Miltie rummaged through the pile. "And one nearly eight months old!" He ran a thick hand through his hair. "Did the circus lose them? Is that why Paddy hasn't opened them?"

"Not according to Dunn." Les jumped up and began pacing. "But, as you know, I really don't trust him. Anyway, he said he didn't really notice anything until one of the acrobats came forward and handed him a bunch of envelopes addressed to my cousin. As I mentioned to you before, Dunn told me he checked with the post office and discovered that Paddy's mail was still being directed to the circus. He says he couldn't find my phone number and admits he hung onto the mail for a while."

Les sighed and slumped back into his chair. "I guess Dunn forgot about it for a while. You remember I told you that my cousin had a best friend who died recently, named Lawrie Agnew?"

Gracie and her uncle nodded, while she poured them all a coffee. Uncle Miltie pushed the sugar in Lester's direction, then Gracie laid down a plate filled with snickerdoodles.

Les spooned sugar into his mug, then continued, "It seems he was in the hospital for a while before he passed away. Anyway, after Agnew's death, somebody at the circus came across an old trunk belonging to him. Dunn said they shipped it to his family in Kentucky."

The others sipped and chewed, patiently waiting for Lester to explain.

"Then, last month, Dunn said he received a pile of mail back from Agnew's family. All addressed to my cousin. It seems they found it in Agnew's trunk." Les gulped his coffee. "I guess there was finally enough mail that even a guy like Dunn had to do something."

Leaning back in his chair, Les waved at the mound of mail scattered across Gracie's kitchen table. "He finally sent it to me."

Gracie pondered Lester's words for a moment. "Do you have any idea what's in the letters?"

"I know," her uncle replied.

They both stared at him.

"Well, I admit I'm guessing, but they look just like the envelopes I receive that contain my benefit check. Don't you think, Gracie?"

She nodded.

"You're right," said Lester. "I phoned them and you know what?"

Again, Gracie and her uncle stared at their guest.

"Paddy hasn't cashed his benefit checks for over six months!"

23

"SIX MONTHS!" Gracie and her uncle simultaneously cried.

"Yeah. Can you believe it?"

"Why would anyone not cash their benefit checks?" asked Uncle Miltie. "I guess I can see forgetting it for a month or so . . . but six? It just doesn't make sense." He arched a pair of bushy eyebrows. "Maybe he's come into some money and doesn't need it?"

Les shook his head. "I don't think so. His clothes are old; the zipper on his suitcase is held together by safety pins. Although he's generous with others, he's actually pretty darned frugal when it comes to himself."

"I guess it's possible he misplaced them," suggested Gracie. "Although it does seem unlikely."

170

Uncle Miltie added, "Why didn't he just go for direct deposit? None of this would have happened."

Her uncle's statement made Gracie sit up in her chair. She suddenly recalled the look of momentary panic in Paddy's face when he and Lester had come over for dinner for the first time. It had happened in response to her uncle asking him almost that very same question.

Uncle Miltie's face brightened. "Hey, remember when I told him about having the government request that I use direct deposit that night you both came to dinner?"

"Yeah," replied Lester. "I guess so."

"Paddy said something like he didn't trust the system, or something. Remember, Gracie?"

But another field of inquiry had popped into Gracie's mind. Instead of answering her uncle, she asked, "Why do you think his mail was found in his friend's trunk?"

The two men exchanged a glance.

"No idea," replied Lester. He noticed the intent expression on Gracie's face. "Do you know?"

Gracie didn't respond immediately. She was allowing her mind to spin freely. A number of situations where Paddy's behavior had puzzled her shimmered into view, one after the other. How did he miss recognizing those two old stamps of her uncle's, especially since one was boldly marked with the words "First Day Issue"?

And now, as she remembered Paddy in the children's hospital room, she wished she had asked him why he had made up the story for Tommy instead of reading the one in his hands.

That brought another image, one of Paddy at Barb's anniversary party. The little man was squinting at the engraving on Barb's piano clock gift, claiming he couldn't read it because he wasn't wearing his glasses.

Another image wisked into her head: that of the Irishman passing off Tommy's storybook to her uncle to read, while he chose to portray the tale in mime. At that moment, Gracie recalled, Paddy didn't mention being without his glasses. No, that time, he immediately handed the book over to her uncle, and suggested that he act out the story while Uncle Miltie read it.

"Gracie?" someone was calling, it seemed from a long way off. "Gracie, are you all right?"

She started at the sound of her uncle's voice. "Oh! Uncle Miltie, Lester," she whispered hoarsely, "I believe I know what's wrong with Paddy."

"What?" they asked in unison.

She paused for a moment, wanting to be certain of her conclusion. After a few seconds, she remained sure. "It's awful. I think the poor man's illiterate."

"What?" Les cried, almost dropping his spoon in surprise. "You think my cousin can't read?"

Gracie nodded, then walked them through her thinking

processes. "You see," she finally added, "it does make some sense. Remember, Les, you told us that Paddy had left home at fourteen?" It was Lester's turn to nod. "You also said he had hated school, and hardly ever went."

"Yeah. I used to envy his having done that as a kid."

Realizing what skipping school may have cost his cousin, Lester suddenly looked aghast.

"Well, if he didn't learn to read in his first few years of school," Gracie continued, "I doubt he'd have had much chance while he was trying to make a living as a clown. After all, when you get past school age, it's pretty difficult to admit something like that."

Lester frowned. "But how did he survive all those years?"

The threesome considered this question for a minute or so.

"I guess you develop coping mechanisms," replied Gracie. "Pretending not to have his glasses or coming up with a plausible excuse to ask someone else to help out. I'm sure it can't have been easy. He probably had some help."

Lester stared at her.

"I think I know," Uncle Miltie replied. He looked across at his niece. "That's why you were wondering about Paddy's mail ending up in Agnew's trunk, right?"

"Right. Remember the circus owner said Paddy's friend had died about six months ago?"

"*Uh huh.*" Lester pursed his lips in thought, then gave up. "Sorry, I'm not following you."

Gracie looked at her uncle. He waved her on. "Well, you said that your cousin and Lawrie Agnew were friends for a long time. I think this Agnew fellow probably helped Paddy out all along."

Her uncle added, "That's why Paddy's mail was in his trunk."

Lester was starting to understand. "And why his checks haven't been cashed for all these last months."

Gracie took a sip, then grimaced, realizing her coffee was cold. She pushed the mug aside, and offered, "I bet the money from the last one processed by the bank, went into Paddy's account just before Lawrie Agnew passed away."

They all sat, each silently thinking about a lifetime of illiteracy. Gracie tried to imagine what it must be like, not being able to experience the joy of rereading a letter from her son, Elmo, or losing herself in one of her favorite mysteries, or even scanning the good old *Mason County Gazette* for news about her beloved town. It made her heart sick. *Thank You, Lord, for giving Paddy one good and true friend. At least, he had someone who was watching out for him down here. No wonder he's at a loss and feeling very down. He thinks he's all alone, still protecting a shameful secret he's carried for decades.*

She looked at the two men, so different in age and temperament. But, at this moment, they were wearing identical expressions of genuine concern for Paddy O'Brien. The sickening feeling in her stomach disappeared, replaced by a warm and encouraging glow. *That's why You brought him to Willow Bend, isn't it? Well, it took us a while to discover what You expected of us. But now, please, don't worry about him any more. He's got us now.*

Lester spoke first. "Wow, I can't imagine not being able to read!" A shocked look crossed his face. "Do . . . do you think he can write?"

Gracie offered hesitantly, "I doubt very much other than his name."

"I bet his friend Agnew made sure he could do that," said Uncle Miltie. "That's one thing no one can survive without. Not in this day and age when a signature is required for practically everything."

"What do you think I should do?" Lester asked. He slid back dejectedly in his seat. "I mean, how do you tell someone like Paddy that you know he can't read?"

"That's a tough one, Les," Uncle Miltie replied. "He's obviously been trying to hide his illiteracy all his life. I think it's important that we remember that he sure hasn't asked us for help."

"I know. He's probably too embarrassed to tell anyone, but now I'm worried about him more than ever. For one thing, I know he's not getting his proper income. Who knows what other benefits he might be missing out on?"

"I think this illiteracy issue has hurt your cousin more deeply than just in the pocketbook," replied Gracie, her tone somber. She glanced between the pair. "If our suppositions are right, Paddy has recently lost his dearest friend, a man he's known for decades and probably the only person to understand his most private shortcoming. I don't think Paddy's been able to grieve for Lawrie Agnew. Not properly. Because, to do so, he might have to reveal his secret."

She glanced out the window and sighed. "No wonder he's lost his ability to smile and is no longer interested in being a circus clown. Trying to entertain everyone else must be impossible, given that he's brokenhearted inside. Worse, he doesn't know how to ask for assistance."

"Someone's got to help him," Les said urgently. "He's gone to see Paul, but I don't think they got very far."

Remembering what Paddy had told her about his conversation with their young pastor, Gracie agreed. "He said that Paul was kind. He also mentioned educated. Perhaps Paddy just couldn't bear to admit to being illiterate to someone like Paul. It's never easy to admit a problem, and it can be harder to admit it to a much younger person."

"Amen to that," replied her uncle.

"He might talk to you, Gracie," urged Lester. "He thinks the world of you."

"He's right, dear," offered Uncle Miltie. "We've seen from the start that he's got a soft spot where you're concerned."

Gracie had to admit that they had a point, but was still uneasy. "Maybe so, but is it our business to broach the subject?" She grimaced. "He's in such a lot of pain as it is. I'm just not sure that I'm the right one to cause him more."

Lester held up several unopened benefit envelopes. "He can't go on like this, Gracie. In pain and not receiving what he's due. We already know he won't accept Paul's counsel. When I try to get him to open up, he just changes the subject. He's just going to get worse if we don't do something."

He looked at Gracie, his eyes pleading. "Please, Gracie, if you don't talk to him, who will? It doesn't have to be today or anything—I know you've got the council meeting tonight—but soon?"

Gracie nodded. "Okay, I'll give it a try in a day or so, if I can find the right circumstances. I'd prefer to take a little time and seek some advice. Perhaps even make a few calls and see if there are any literacy programs available. If Paddy does talk to me, I'd like to be able to tell him what help is available.

"But I can't make any promises, Les. It might make things worse for your cousin."

"I guess that's just a risk we have to take." He looked at her gratefully.

"Thank you! My prayers are with you, Gracie. I just know he'll respond to you, and when he finds out that we can help him, he's bound to find his smile again."

Gracie nodded slightly. *Well, Lord, I'm really going to need Your advice this time. I have no idea how to broach this difficult subject. I sure don't want to make Paddy's life more miserable than it already is.*

She listened hard, but heard nothing. Okay, she thought, this is something I'm going to have to do instinctively. When the last word popped into her head, she smiled inside. It was too much of a coincidence.

You are with me, dear God, aren't You?

THAT AFTERNOON, GRACIE made some last minute calls to the coalition members who had offered to assist her at the council meeting. Everyone was prepared except Phil Murphy.

"I've borrowed the sound equipment from the high school, so that's all set. But I'm not sure what we should use as our example," he said.

"Well," replied Gracie, "something that's instantly recognizable to most people would be best. I think a classic is the only choice."

"Great, but which one?" Phil then offered a couple of suggestions.

"*Hmm*, I'm not sure I'd call those classics, Phil." She paused for a moment and made a recommendation.

Gooseberry slipped into the living room. Instead of joining

her on the couch, however, the big cat leapt onto one of the wing chairs. After a circling for a moment, he settled himself inside the puddle of afternoon light, which poured in through the picture window.

"Perfect! And you know what? I think I know just where to find a copy. Thanks, Gracie. See you, tonight."

The high school band director rang off.

Gracie sighed with relief. Now that the arrangements for the evening were all set, her thoughts turned to helping Lester's cousin. She pulled the phone book within reach and began rifling through it. Would *L* for literacy help? At the same time, she let her mind roam. Surely she must know someone locally who could help point her in the right direction.

After a second or two, she paused. Of course! Pat Allen's sister, Emily Wicks, worked as a county family services social worker. Although Emily didn't live in Willow Bend, Gracie had met her several times at church events, when she had accompanied her sister, Pat. Gracie had even requested Emily's assistance on occasion. She was certain that Emily would know where to find help for Paddy O'Brien.

It didn't take her long to locate Emily's number. Fortunately, the social worker answered on the second ring.

"Oh, hello, Gracie!" Emily exclaimed in surprise. "What a funny coincidence. My sister was just telling me about you and your coalition when she phoned a couple of nights ago. What a fine thing you're doing!"

"Thank you, Emily," replied Gracie. "I appreciate your support, but I'm not calling about the audio book petition."

"Oh?" Emily Wicks paused, and her tone turned professional. "Do you know someone who needs the help of Family Services?"

"Yes, that's why I called. Well ... actually, I'm not really sure if Family Services is the correct department."

"That's fine. Why don't you tell me the problem and then I can let you know if we're the right ones to call."

"Okay, thank you. Have you met Lester Twomley? He's in our choir."

"Is he the short one? Sings tenor?"

Gracie smiled. "That's him."

"Has something gone wrong? I can't imagine Lester needing Family Services."

"No, no, not Lester," Gracie replied quickly. "It's his much older cousin, Paddy, I'm worried about. You see, Emily, I'm afraid that Paddy O'Brien is illiterate."

"Oh dear! What a shame! Are you certain he can't read or write?"

"Well, no, not really, but it's the only thing that makes sense given the circumstances." Gracie then quickly provided Emily with some background on Paddy, his vocation and recent job loss, and finally why she believed he was illiterate.

It took a while for Gracie to finish. Emily listened carefully, then waited for a moment to process the information. "I see.

I've been helping people of all types and occupations for many years, Gracie, but I have to admit I've never met a real clown. I think though that I'd like to very much. Have you spoken to—it's Paddy, is it?"

"Yes, Paddy O'Brien. A very sweet man. As to speaking to him about it . . . well, it's a little complicated. You see, Emily, when he came to visit Lester, he was very depressed and unwilling to talk. He wouldn't explain why he had lost his job, in fact, he wouldn't talk about the circus at all. But Lester got the impression that Paddy's heart was simply no longer in entertaining children. That shocked and worried him as his cousin had always loved being a performer and prided himself on his ability to make kids laugh."

Emily interjected, "That does sound like someone who's been through a traumatic experience. We must remember that even clowns have real lives and have to cope with the same sort of personal, family and work issues as the rest of us."

"Yes. It sounds a little odd, given that Paddy's workplace was a circus, doesn't it? But of course it's true," replied Gracie. "And you're right about him being in distress. I invited Les and Paddy both to dinner, and it was immediately obvious to everyone at the table when they first met him that Paddy was suffering emotionally."

"Yes, that makes sense. You see, Gracie, adults with low literacy skills certainly experience a lot of shame, frustration and fear. You believe this is what's troubling Paddy?"

Gracie thought for a second. "Well, not entirely, no. From what Les has told me, his cousin's behavior has only recently changed. Now, if we're correct about his being unable to read or write, then that's a problem Paddy has struggled with for decades."

Gracie sighed. "No, I believe it's something traumatic, just as you suggested. And I do know that Paddy O'Brien's world was recently turned upside down. We just discovered that he lost a dear friend six months ago."

"That's certainly bad enough."

"I agree, Emily. But I worry because I fear he's too embarrassed to ask for help and have someone discover his secret."

Emily exhaled heavily. "The poor man. He's not alone, you know. There are thousands of adults in Indiana who can't read."

"My goodness!" exclaimed Gracie. "I never imagined that the problem was so widespread!"

"Sadly, it is. And the toll isn't only personal. It affects us all, costing our country millions a year from accidents at the workplace, lost tax revenues and decreased productivity."

The social worker's voice lightened. "The good news is that you're never too old to learn how to read and write. Tell me, has Paul Meyer approached Paddy?"

"No, but Lester encouraged Paddy to visit him. They did talk, it just wasn't very successful. Paddy told me himself that he couldn't speak freely to Paul."

"It sounds like Paddy might talk to you."

Gracie breathed deeply. "That's what my uncle and Les think and why I've called you. I was hoping to get some advice before I try broaching the subject with Paddy."

"I'm glad you called, Gracie. There's a lot of help and information available."

Gracie's sigh of relief was audible. "Thank you, Emily. I appreciate any advice you can give me."

"First, let me find you a few names and numbers. Indiana has a variety of places to go: literacy foundations and resource centers with reading and writing programs, helplines, information on web sites, conferences, newsletters—all kinds of help. Just hang on a second or so while I pull them up on my computer."

A couple of minutes later, Gracie was jotting down the contact information for two adult learning programs in the area, plus several Web site addresses.

"Now," Emily continued, "all that stuff will help you once you've got Paddy to admit to his problem. But to do that. . ."

"Yes. That's the part that really worries me, Emily. After all, why would he admit his illiteracy to me?"

"Because he wants to. No, even more than that, Gracie, he needs to." Emily's voice became stronger. "If he's mourning for his friend, as you suggested, then he's already going to be in a fragile, emotional state. Grieving is difficult, it saps a person of their strength, of their spirit, sometimes tragically of their will to live. Now, if you're right, your poor friend is also trying to cope with a second, longer-standing obstacle."

Emily paused to inhale. "Let me tell you, it's not easy to keep a secret at the best of times, in the best of health. Especially for over sixty years! Concealing something from the world takes a lot of energy, and willpower. Frankly, I don't think Paddy has enough vitality and stamina to cope much longer with both of his problems. He's going to want to talk, to free himself of the burdens of grief, shame and frustration."

"I hope so. I feel so sorry for him. What do you suggest I do?"

"In my experience, troubled people often break down in the face of another's torment; usually it's someone they know and care for. I realize that Paddy is new to Willow Bend so he may not have yet developed a close enough relationship. I don't know, but from what you've told me, I believe he's very close to the edge. I don't think it will take much longer for him to ask for help."

Then Emily sighed. "So, in answer to your question, I guess all I can suggest at this moment is that you try and be there for him. Let him know that you care, and that you're ready to listen."

"Thank you so much, Emily, for the advice and for all the information on literacy programs," said Gracie. "I'm so glad I called. At least now, I feel prepared."

"That's good. Don't hesitate to call me again if you need anything else. Oh, and one last thing."

"Yes?"

"Remember our dear Lord's words, as told to us by St. James? 'Behold we account them blessed who have endured'?"

Gracie paused, thinking. "Oh, now I remember. Yes."

Emily added, "St. James also said to be patient."

Gracie smiled, recalling the passage. ". . . the patience of Job, right?"

"Now you *are* prepared. Good luck, Gracie. Be sure and let me know how it all turns out."

YOU'VE ALL SEEN OUR PETITION and noted the hundreds of signatures supporting our request to have you review your recent decision to reduce the funds allocated to the library," Gracie said, raising her voice so that everyone in the room could hear. "So you're aware that a lot of residents of Willow Bend are against what you've done."

"And if there's any chance they don't get it," Roy Bell shouted, "we're all here to make sure they do!"

"We're aware, yes," Mayor Ritter responded with a forced smile. As though in demonstration of his understanding, he patted the stack of sign-up sheets piled in front of him. A couple of council members nodded understandingly. The others seated at the head table looked around warily.

It wasn't often that town council meetings in Willow Bend were packed. However, a couple hundred residents had rushed through their evening meal in order to attend this particular assembly. Most had found seats; however, a dozen or so teenagers lined the walls, along with several staffers from the *Gazette*, including Rocky Gravino.

The audience had been quiet for over an hour, forced to sit through a review of the last meeting's minutes and discussions on several unrelated issues, but they were now becoming restless. The mayor had given Gracie the floor to make her presentation on behalf of the coalition only seconds before they might have taken it by force.

Gracie stood at the front of the crowd, facing the table of elected members. She glanced at her uncle, who sat in the front row, alongside Anna and Joe Searfoss. Uncle Miltie raised a thumb in salute.

"That's good," Gracie said, "but what you don't know is how it's going to feel to not be able to borrow audio books from our library." Gracie looked at each council member in turn, then shifted her gaze to the audience. "Honestly, I don't think many of us can really imagine that situation. You see, for most of us, who are healthy and strong, listening to an audio book is merely an occasional pleasure. Something to pass the time on a long road trip or one of several ways to take a break from our stressful lives."

She swung back to the council members. "If audio books weren't available, it wouldn't be a huge loss. We have other ways to entertain ourselves: written books, television, movies, crossward puzzles, any number of outdoor activities such as golfing or weeding a garden. That's because we have both the physical health and the financial means to participate. We're really not the ones being hurt by your decision."

Gracie glanced over at Paul Meyer, who stood near a row of light switches at the main door. Her eyes then slid to the back of the room where Kenneth Ebersole and Susie Frantz stood by the windows. Finally, her gaze rested on Phil Murphy, who stood in front of a small table. He held up a tiny flashlight in acknowledgment.

"So with your kind indulgence, this evening the members of the Audio Books Coalition would like to try and give you some idea of what it's like to be someone for whom audio books are a lifeline, not merely an indulgence."

Tom Ritter held up his hands. "Okay, Gracie." He glanced at the council members.

One man was frowning. "I want to state my opposition to this stunt. I think it's ridiculous of us to tolerate it."

"What do you know?" a voice called out.

The man's frown deepened.

Ritter held up his hands for quiet, then glanced at the woman taking notes. "So noted, that Allen Young objects. However, the majority agreed to this, so go ahead, Gracie. The floor is still yours."

"Thank you, Mr. Mayor." Gracie turned to the two men at the back and nodded. Phil and Ken quickly tugged the blinds closed, shutting out all exterior light. She glanced at Paul.

The lights snapped off. Suddenly, the council chamber was pitch black.

A hiss of whispers filled the room.

"Please!" called out Gracie. "May I ask that everyone remain very quiet. This won't last too long." The noises faded. "Thank you. Now, Mayor Ritter and esteemed council members, imagine that this is what you see every waking minute."

"You mean, we're to pretend that we are blind?" a councilwoman's voice asked.

"Yes, that's exactly the experience we're trying to create. Now, could you also imagine that you're in a bed, unable to get up on your own? You're completely dependent on someone else to help you. Perhaps a nurse or a daughter."

The room's occupants sat still, listening. Only a few murmurs and rustling noises punctuated the silence.

"That's right," Gracie said. "No more talking. We're halfway through already. Now, I'm going to ask everyone to remain very quiet for one minute. Starting now."

Gracie began counting to sixty in her head, using a technique she learned from her grandson. *One elephant, two elephants, three elephants....*

Fifteen seconds passed. A woman coughed.

At thirty seconds, a number of people seemed to feel a need to shift noisily in their chairs. The tension in the blackness was palpable.

26

GRACIE WAS JUST HITTING FIFTY when a cell phone buzzed.

"Turn it off!" a woman hissed.

After a panicked fumble, the room was silent again.

Gracie finally reached sixty. "Okay, the minute's up."

Several people sighed in relief.

Gracie waited until quiet resumed. "Now, before I ask Paul to turn on the lights, I want the council members to remember how it felt to be isolated, in the dark, and unable to get up, *for just sixty seconds.*"

"And then, try and imagine what it must be like to spend an hour or more a day like that. With nothing or no one to break the loneliness or the monotony. Good. Now, if you would humor me for a little bit longer and just listen."

A number of seconds passed. Gracie could feel the anxiety rebuilding. A light flared briefly, then vanished.

Suddenly, from the back, rose a deep voice. A couple of people cried out in surprise, but were quickly shushed by their neighbors. After half a minute, it was obvious that they were all listening to a man with a charming southern accent reading from *The Adventures of Huckleberry Finn*.

Immediately, the atmosphere in the dark room lightened. Though she couldn't see anyone, Gracie imagined in front of her eager facial expressions and people leaning forward in anticipation of the next word. She waited a minute longer, knowing that everyone was listening intently.

"Okay, Phil. Thanks."

The light flickered again and the beautiful voice stopped.

"*Ohhh,*" moaned the crowd in disappointment.

"Turn it back on!" a man's voice urged.

A teenager shouted. "Yeah. I was just getting into it. What's it called, anyway?"

Several citizens groaned.

A man's voice snapped peevishly, "Good grief! Don't you kids learn anything in school? Haven't you heard of Huck Finn?"

Gracie called above the din, "Lights, please, Paul!"

The room seemed to shimmer with light. Many people shielded their eyes, while others stood and stretched. Gracie caught Paddy O'Brien's eye. He was sitting beside Lester Twomley, near the doorway. With a lopsided smile, he clapped silently in appreciation. She was pleased to see his continued interest in the petition.

The mayor and the council members were all watching Gracie. She could see the point of her demonstration becoming clear as they sat there, thinking.

"Given what you've just experienced," said Gracie, "are you still comfortable with your earlier decision to reduce the library's funding?"

For a moment, the council members said nothing.

"That was a very useful experiment," Ann O'Neill finally commented. "I think you've made your point quite clearly."

Two of her fellow members nodded emphatically.

Even Allen Young, who had earlier dismissed Gracie's effort as a stunt, nodded begrudgingly. "Guess I underestimated the effectiveness of what you were trying to do."

The mayor glanced under some papers for his gavel. Unable to locate it, he rapped the table top with his fist. "So, we now appreciate," Tom Ritter began, "more than ever before, the value of audio books to a very select percentage of the population."

"And very vulnerable, let's not forget," added Ruth Stefano.

Tom Ritter conceded her point with a slight dip of his head. "I believe it's important to state that this council did not instruct the library administration to stop funding the purchase of audio books. That was not our decision."

"Come on, now, Mr. Mayor, that's just semantics," Don Delano stood up to say. "Surely you don't expect this audience to buy that old argument?"

Tom Ritter looked uncomfortable.

Don remained standing. "The library's administration was just following this town council's orders to cut back. You can't try and pass on the blame to them."

"He's right!" Roy Bell hollered. "The buck stops right here, with you folks. And don't you forget it!"

Cheers filled the room.

The mayor held up both hands. "Okay. Fair enough, but our fiscal problem still exists. Our hands remain tied. We have to make cuts in our budget, that's unavoidable. You don't like our previous approach. That's all and well and good . . . but how are we going to keep within our budgets, and at the same time reinstate the funds necessary for the library's purchase of audio books?"

He paused for effect. "It's not an easy question, I know. Anybody got an idea to put forward?"

"Why don't you all take a cut in salary?" one man offered, his voice sharp with sarcasm.

Half of the audience clapped enthusiastically.

The mayor waved a palm. "*Realistic* ideas, friends, please."

Roy Bell stood. "Well, maybe there's another program that could be cut or reduced a little."

The council members frowned as one. Ann O'Neill raised a hand. "Of course, that's a possibility. However, as Mayor Ritter explained earlier, we undertook a careful review of the services and programs offered by the town. And after a great deal of discussion, we had to make some tough decisions."

Bell snapped. "That's what we pay you for!"

"Indeed," Ann continued smoothly, "but that's exactly what brought us all here tonight." She stood. "What I'm trying to say, sir, is that it's not going to be easy to find the necessary funds. Cutting another program or service will most likely result in more complaints and dissatisfaction."

Allen Young cleared his throat and became the next council member to join the fray. "It seems to me that if these services are so important to you folks, perhaps you should be willing to pay more taxes to cover their costs."

The room echoed with cries of "outrageous!" Then, a number of attendees jumped to their feet, speaking simultaneously.

"More taxes?!" squealed an elderly man.

"No way!" chorused the teenagers.

A young woman with a baby in her arms shouted, "You've got to be kidding! We're already taxed to the max, as it is."

Phil Murphy called out from the back. "I thought you said realistic ideas, Mr. Mayor."

"I did," Ritter replied. "And I'm still waiting to hear one."

Councilwoman Stefano rose. "I have a recommendation."

THE NOISE LEVEL SANK to a disgruntled murmur.

The mayor shot an appreciative look at Ruth Stefano, then urged her on. "By all means."

She took a breath. "I think I speak for all the council members in saying we've learned a valuable lesson in the democratic process here tonight."

A man wearing wire-framed glasses leapt to his feet. "Oh, no, not another useless speech!"

Gracie held up a hand. "Please, let her finish."

He started to reply, then paused. "If you say so, Mrs. Parks," he replied, before slumping back in his seat.

Smiling tightly, Ruth Stefano continued, "Thank you, Gracie." She looked directly at her heckler. "I'm sorry, I didn't mean to make a speech. What I meant to say is that your attendance here tonight, along with everyone else's, sends us council members a powerful message."

She turned her focus to the whole audience. "You want to be heard, and have every right. I suggest that we do just that by recommending that we strike a committee as soon as possible—"

A woman near the door moaned.

"Not another committee!" called out a frustrated-sounding voice.

Ruth Stefano interjected quickly. "No, not just *any* committee, but one with representatives from you as well as from the council, with a clear mandate and time frame. Together, perhaps, we can work as a team to discover ways to solve our funding problems."

She paused. "That is, unless any of you has a better idea? That's why we're here now, folks, so please, let us know."

For the first time since Gracie's experiment had plunged them into darkness, the audience was silent.

Cordelia Fountain struggled to her feet. "Who's going to represent us citizens?"

A chorus of voices immediately shouted, "Gracie Parks!"

Uncle Miltie waved one of his canes in support. Anna and Joe clasped hands and waved. Gracie glanced at them affectionately.

A ripple of applause built quickly into a roaring wave. "Yes! Gracie! Gracie!"

Ruth Stefano smiled and looked at Gracie. "Would you be willing to participate?" she asked, attempting to be heard over the din.

Gracie silently prayed for support, then replied, "Yes." Her voice was strong and clear.

Applause welled up from every corner.

"Well, done, Gracie!" Kenneth Ebersole called out.

It took Tom Ritter several attempts to regain order. By the time the audience settled down, his palm was as pink from pounding as his face was from shouting. "Quiet, please. Quiet! Thank you, Councilwoman Stefano, for your recommendation. And thank you, Mrs. Parks for agreeing to participate."

Now his listeners were calming down. Mayor Ritter looked around. "Remember," he said, "this isn't a question of winning or losing. It's about providing the services our town needs in the most effective and economical manner possible."

His audience listened intently.

Ritter glanced at the large clock hanging on the back wall. "It's nearly ten. I believe we've made a lot of progress tonight. Since we've all agreed on the new committee, I propose Councilwoman Stefano be named as the chair. I also propose that she and Mrs. Parks get together in the next few days and decide who else should be involved."

"That okay with you, Ruth?"

She nodded.

"Mrs. Parks?"

"Yes, Mayor, thank you."

"Thank you. Okay, last thing, how about we suggest that anyone interested in working on this committee give either Ruth or Gracie a call?"

Mayor Ritter addressed the recording secretary. "Please note, as usual, that our next meeting is in two weeks."

She nodded.

"Fine. We'll expect Ruth Stefano to have appointed the other committee members by then. Do you think you might also be able to provide us with your mandate and time frame for decisions, by then?"

Ruth glanced questioningly at Gracie, who nodded slightly. "I think that's possible, yes," she told him.

"Excellent. Meeting adjourned. Thank you all." His face wore an expression of relief.

By the time Gracie, her uncle and Marge arrived at home, they were all talked out. Gracie was relieved to have the few minutes of silence. She couldn't help but silently wonder whether there was any chance her new committee wouldn't be a waste of time. She also debated whether she might have taken on too much responsibility.

"Penny?" asked Marge, looking concerned. It wasn't like her friend Gracie to keep so mum.

"I was just worrying about the committee," Gracie sighed. "Whether we'll actually be able to do any better than the council. Tom was right. There have to be cuts somewhere and therefore there'll always be new problems."

"Maybe, but what's your choice?" Marge said. "It seems to me that the public, as represented by you and the committee, now has a chance to actively participate. That in itself is positive. If nothing else, you're breaking ground, Gracie. I don't think our municipal decision-making process is ever going to be the same."

"She's right," Uncle Miltie contributed. "Today, too few folks even vote, much less take the time to personally let their elected leaders know what they're thinking."

His voice rose. "You're setting a fine example for everyone, my girl, but especially for those young folks in attendance tonight. You've proven that the public can and should be heard."

He looked thoughtful for an instant. "You know, Gracie? It might be a great thing to have one of those kids on the committee. What do you think?"

"It's an excellent idea! I'll suggest it to Ruth tomorrow."

At that moment, Gooseberry came wandering in, curious to know what his humans were doing in the kitchen, hoping, as usual, that it involved offering him a treat.

"Well, Gooseberry," Uncle Miltie addressed him genially.

"Your mistress is the woman of the hour hereabouts, and we're pretty proud of her. What do *you* think?"

"*Meow.*"

28

TWO MORNINGS LATER, Gracie came upon Paddy
O'Brien sitting alone outside Tommy Hartzell's hospital room. Down the hall, she spied a couple pacing the tile
hallway. She recognized the man as Vic Hartzell. She immediately sent a prayer of hope and strength heavenward for him
and his wife, who was clutching his hand. And for Tommy,
too.

Paddy's sad expression lifted a bit when he saw her
approaching. "Good morning, Gracie," he whispered. "What
brings you here?"

She settled into the seat beside him. Then she handed him
a large envelope. "You do. I called Lester's earlier, looking for
you. He told me that Tommy's surgery was scheduled for this
morning and that I might find you here. Have you heard any
news?"

Paddy shook his head. "He's still in recovery. I'm not sure when he'll be back." His eyes went to the Hartzells. "Poor things. It's been a long wait."

"They haven't given up hope, have they?"

Paddy rubbed his eyes. "'Hope is the thing with feathers, That perches in the soul,'" he began softly. "'And sings the tune without the words, And never stops—at all.'"

Gracie stared at him. "Why, that's so haunting and beautiful. Did you write it?"

"Me?" His green eyes widened. "Oh, no. That's Emily Dickinson. Do you know her?"

Hiding the astonishment she felt to find the man she believed to be illiterate quoting the legendary nineteenth-century poet, Gracie nodded. "She's one of my favorites. I just didn't know those lines."

"My friend Lawrie's, too. He used to quote her all the time." He was quickly silent, as though he had revealed too much.

"Lester told me Mr. Agnew passed away six months ago. I'm so sorry for your loss," Gracie replied gently. "I know what it's like to grieve. It's very hard."

He tensed, and Gracie feared he would tell her it was none of her business.

After a long moment, though, Paddy turned to her, his bottom lip quivering. "Thank you. Lawrie was a fighter, just like Tommy. It took him a long time to give in, even though he was in the hospital for the last month or so."

He glanced around. "That's why I hate these places so much." Paddy slowly shook his head. "Letting good people die is God's cruel joke, don't you think?"

Gracie slowly shook her head. "Paddy, I don't believe God is ever cruel."

"He...He let my best mate die. He's allowed this dear little lad to be blind. Isn't that cruel?"

"I don't pretend to understand everything that happens in His divine creation. He does work in mysterious ways, ways that are beyond our understanding. But deliberately cruel? Never. And you must understand that death is part of life."

Paddy looked at the floor. "I just wasn't expecting it. I wasn't ready to lose Lawrie. We'd buried his wife a few years earlier. That was hard enough." He looked up at her. "You lost your husband, didn't you? Les told me about him, how well-loved he was—by everyone."

By now, Gracie was usually able to control her emotions when she talked about Elmo's death. Something about being in the harsh light of the hospital heightened her memories, however, and she surprised herself by having to fight back tears. After a minute, she managed to whisper, "He was killed in a car accident." She paused. "I don't think anyone is ready to lose a loved one. Ever."

Paddy stood and disappeared into Tommy's room. Gracie's envelope slid to the floor. Returning quickly, Paddy offered her a box of tissues, then stooped to retrieve the envelope.

"What's in here then?"

"They belong to you. Your cousin brought them to me."

Paddy pulled out several unopened pieces of mail. "You. Why? These are *my* letters." His expression hardened. "He had no right."

"Of course he did!" Gracie retorted. "For one thing, there are uncashed Social Security checks!" She paused, regaining control, then added gently, "Oh, Paddy, it's obvious you're not receiving your proper benefits. Lester's worried for you. Can't you understand that?"

Hastily, he jammed the envelopes back inside. "No one asked him to."

Gracie half-smiled. "No one needs to be asked to try and help someone they care about."

"Why did he bring them to you, then? Why didn't he just come to me?"

"Perhaps he should have, Paddy, but he was afraid to embarrass you."

"Embarrass me?" Paddy's eyes flickered between the letters and Gracie with growing comprehension. Finally, he hung his head. "You know, don't you?" he added, so softly that Gracie barely heard.

GRACIE'S RESPONSE was filled with compassion. "That you are unable to read and write? Yes, Paddy, I know."

Paddy covered his face with his hands. "Oh, what you must think of me!"

Gracie reached out and touched his arm. "Dear Paddy O'Brien, I think you are a kind, generous and brave man, who's spent his life making families laugh."

He looked up at her in disbelief. "You . . . you do?" He grabbed the envelope, ripped free a letter and tore it open. Thrusting it toward Gracie, he said, "It's become a living nightmare."

He held up another letter. "Without Lawrie to read for me, I have no idea what this says." He let the mail fall to the floor. "Or any of it! Isn't that stupid? He was the only one who could help me and now he's gone! He handled my money, read and answered all my mail for me. Without him, I'm so lost."

He gave a deep sigh. "You don't know what it's like, Gracie, not being able to figure out the simplest words. Feeling so stupid! Making up stories to explain why you didn't see that article in the newspaper or why you haven't read the latest book. Always worried about being found out and coming up with daft excuses, like not having my glasses or suffering eye strain, or some such malarkey! That's why I didn't catch those old stamps of your uncle's."

"And why you made up the story for Tommy."

He turned to her, his eyes glistening in pain. "Why, little children can read and write better than me!"

"Paddy, being unable to read or write is nothing to be ashamed of."

"That's easy for you to say."

"Perhaps. But I can tell you what is truly shameful."

He looked at her curiously. "What?"

"Refusing to admit that you need help, especially when help is readily available."

Turning toward the Hartzells, Paddy replied, "I told Lawrie. That was hard enough. After he . . . he died, I felt so alone. Just didn't know who to turn to."

He stared straight ahead. "That's when everything started to fall apart. I just didn't know how to deal with things—

letters, money, that sort of stuff. I . . . I was too ashamed to ask for help. But that wasn't the worst thing. No, Gracie, the worst thing was that I just couldn't bear to put on the make-up, couldn't see my way to making anyone laugh anymore."

His own brief laugh was bitter. "Some clown, *huh*? Can't even make myself smile, much less a tent full of kiddies. No wonder Mr. Dunn sent me packing."

"You're not alone, you know. There are thousands of adults just here in Indiana who are illiterate. Many of them are getting help, learning to read."

Paddy gave a disbelieving shake of the head. "Thousands?"

She nodded. "There are programs and services designed just for people like you. We can find out all about them if you're interested. I've already learned a lot."

Paddy scratched at a nick in the arm of his chair.

Before either could speak, the sounds of voices and the rattle of medical equipment filled the hallway. Tommy Hartzell was being wheeled back from the recovery room.

His parents rushed up the hall and grabbed for their son's hands. The little boy, whose eyes were swathed in white, cried out at their touch. Gracie and Paddy watched and waited as the orderlies carefully shifted Tommy's small body onto the stationary bed, tucked him in gently, then fiddled with various tubes and monitors before leaving.

After several minutes, Vic Hartzell stepped into the hall. His expression appeared positive. "Tommy's asking for you,

Mr. O'Brien. My wife told him that you've been waiting for him. Would you come say hello, just for a minute?"

Paddy glanced at Gracie. She smiled. He stood and joined the Hartzells at their son's bedside. "I'll wait for you and drive you back to Les's," she told him.

Gracie could see nothing other than the backs of the three adults bending over the boy. A second later, her heart lifted as Tommy's laughter floated toward her.

Paddy rejoined her a few minutes later.

Walking slowly to her car, Gracie asked, "How is he?"

Paddy held up both hands, showing her a set of crossed fingers. "His father said the doctors are optimistic, but they won't know the results for weeks." Paddy held open the driver's door for Gracie. "He's a brilliant lad, that one. He's even got more guts than the Flying Fetisov boys."

He hesitated, then spoke softly, "You know, Gracie, I never thought I would learn something from a seven-year old. But if that wee boy has the courage to face a future without being able to see, then I think I can find it in myself to ask for some help. That is, if you think I'm worth it."

Thank You, dear Lord!

Gracie surprised the older man with a warm hug. "Of course you're worth it! Lester will be so proud of you, Paddy. Just like I am."

Paddy flushed and cleared his throat. "I couldn't have done

it without you, Gracie, and your patience with me. I'm forever in your debt."

They embraced quickly again, then Gracie slipped behind the wheel. Before Paddy closed the door, he added, "Maybe some day I'll be able to read to Tommy." His wrinkled face beamed. "Wouldn't that be a lark!"

Suddenly, his brows knitted. "If only Lawrie were here to—"

She waited until he walked around the car, before asking, "What did you say to make Tommy laugh? I heard him, and felt so proud of you."

Paddy settled into the passenger seat but didn't reply. Maybe he hadn't caught what she'd said.

Gracie started the car and began driving. She remained quiet, letting her passenger think.

Halfway to Lester's house, Paddy tugged something red from his pocket and held it up. It was his clown nose. "I pushed this into Tommy's little hand and told him that if he could tell me what it was, I would come back to the hospital when he was a titch better and put on a real circus show."

Then, Paddy O'Brien thrilled Gracie with a dazzling smile. Not just any smile. For the first time since she had met him, his bright green eyes glowed with happiness. Paddy's whole body seemed alive and brimming with energy, just as Gracie had imagined it should. She was confident that one day, she would see him dance that Irish jig.

"One squeeze and the lad guessed right away!" Paddy chuckled. "Now, I have to figure out a clown routine that both the sighted and the blind can enjoy!"

"That's wonderful, Paddy! The children will love it."

"I sure hope so. After all, I am a little rusty." He turned to face her. "Say, Gracie, do you think Uncle Miltie could be persuaded to dress up like a clown on a regular basis?"

He pretended to play a violin and his feet skipped lightly on the floor. "It sure would be great to have him play my sidekick again."

"Are you kidding, Paddy?" Gracie grinned. "If you're not careful, *you're* the one who'll be playing second fiddle to my uncle!"

Gracie's Broccoli Salad

- ✓ 2 bunches broccoli, trimmed to florets with 1 inch of stem
- ✓ Juice and grated rind of 1/2 lemon
- ✓ 1/2 cup olive oil
- ✓ 1 tablespoon red wine vinegar
- ✓ 1/2 tablespoon chopped parsley
- ✓ 5 anchovy filets, finely chopped
- ✓ 1/2 teaspoon garlic
- ✓ 1/2 teaspoon Dijon-style mustard
- ✓ Freshly ground pepper

Cook broccoli for four minutes in boiling water to which lemon juice and rind have been added. Drain it well and run under cold water, then refrigerate. Now mix the other ingredients together in a jar and shake well. Put the broccoli in a bowl and pour the dressing over it, tossing gently to mix. Let it sit, covered with plastic wrap, at room temperature for one hour before serving.

Gracie says, "I suggest watching over the cooking broccoli and using a wooden spoon to keep it pressed down into the water. This way the pieces all cook evenly."

About the Author

NICOLA FURLONG makes every effort to steal time away from cycling, playing ice hockey, growing perennials from seed and devouring chocolates (mostly devouring chocolates) to slip a snippet of mystery and suspense writing into each day.

Born in Edmonton, Alberta, the sixth of eight children, Nicola was raised in the Canadian provinces of Saskatchewan, Ontario and Prince Edward Island. She received a degree in fine arts and psychology from Carleton University in Ottawa, and then, following several older siblings, scrambled up the bureaucratic ladder with the Canadian government. After the publication of a number of essays, articles and short stories, her first mystery novel, *Teed Off!*, was published in 1996. Later that year, she left the civil service behind to concentrate on writing fiction and also to serve as a consultant to fisheries and environmental organizations. Her second novel, *A Hemorrhaging of Souls*, was published in 1998. She recently finished a suspense thriller entitled *Thy Will Be Done* and is currently researching a sequel.

Nicola lives in Sidney-by-the-Sea, a small town on southern Vancouver Island, British Columbia. You can visit Nicola's Web site at www.nicolafurlong.com.

A NOTE FROM THE EDITORS

This original Guideposts Book was created by the Books and Inspirational Media Division of the company that publishes *Guideposts*, a monthly magazine filled with true stories of hope and inspiration.

Guideposts is available by subscription. All you have to do is write to Guideposts, 39 Seminary Hill Road, Carmel, New York 10512. When you subscribe, each month you can count on receiving exciting new evidence of God's presence, His guidance and His limitless love for all of us.

Guideposts Books are available on the World Wide Web at www.guidepostsbooks.com. Follow our popular book of devotionals, *Daily Guideposts*, and read excerpts from some of our best-selling books. You can also send prayer requests to our Monday morning Prayer Fellowship and read stories from recent issues of our magazines, *Guideposts, Angels on Earth,* and *Guideposts for Teens.*